A plan gone wrong . . .

Smells Orville recognized from chemistry class singed his nose. Smoke began to burn his eyes.

"Keep calm, everyone," a Placid teacher called. "Exit the bleachers row by row. Then make your way calmly to the back of the parking lot."

Orville slipped out of his seat and hurried away from the bleachers.

"Ugh! It smells like rotten eggs," Kit complained as they made their way to the exit.

"More like cow poop," Stu added.

"Ohhh, it's terrible!" Edmundo moaned.

Agatha held her nose and made her way out of the stadium. She didn't say a word until they had reached the back of the parking lot. "Orville," she whispered. "Trixie's flames were aimed toward that field house. Could *we* have started that fire?"

Lissa stepped up next to her. "Hey! I thought you said our prank was safe," she cried.

"Orville, tell me," ████████████████ do that?"

The **Wright &**
Wong Mysteries

Wright & Wong

The Case of the Prank that Stank

Laura J. Burns & Melinda Metz

SLEUTH
RAZORBILL

Wright & Wong 1: The Case of the Prank that Stank

RAZORBILL

Published by the Penguin Group
Penguin Young Readers Group
345 Hudson Street, New York, New York 10014, U.S.A.
Penguin Group (USA) Inc., 375 Hudson Street, New York, New York 10014, U.S.A.
Penguin Books Canada Ltd, 10 Alcorn Avenue, Toronto, Ontario,
Canada M4V 3B2 (a division of Pearson Penguin Canada, Inc.)
Penguin Books Ltd, 80 Strand, London WC2R 0RL, England
Penguin Ireland, 25 St Stephen's Green, Dublin 2, Ireland
(a division of Penguin Books Ltd)
Penguin Group (Australia), 250 Camberwell Road, Camberwell,
Victoria 3124, Australia (a division of Pearson Australia Group Pty Ltd)
Penguin Books India Pvt Ltd, 11 Community Centre, Panchsheel Park,
New Delhi – 110 017, India
Penguin Group (NZ), Cnr Airborne and Rosedale Roads, Albany, Auckland 1310,
New Zealand (a division of Pearson New Zealand Ltd)
Penguin Books (South Africa) (Pty) Ltd, 24 Sturdee Avenue, Rosebank,
Johannesburg 2196, South Africa

Penguin Books Ltd, Registered Offices: 80 Strand, London WC2R 0RL, England

10 9 8 7 6 5 4 3 2 1

Interior design by Christopher Grassi

Library of Congress Cataloging-in-Publication Data is available

Printed in the United States of America

Wright & Wong

The Case of the Prank that Stank

Chapter 1

"Don't even say it," Agatha Wong warned her best friend, Orville Wright.

"But Agatha—" Orville began.

She held out her hand. "Just give me the tape."

Agatha studied the bright green flyer she'd just smacked onto the telephone pole. She wanted to be sure it was straight. The flyer advertised midnight boat rides around the lake of her town—Bottomless Lake, Arizona. Boat rides during which Trixie, the legendary Bottomless Lake monster, might be spotted.

Agatha nudged the right-hand corner of the flyer up a bit and applied a piece of masking tape. "There." She smiled. "Straighter than Cousin Lee's hair."

"Agatha—" Orville tried again.

"I know, I know," Agatha said as they continued down the sidewalk toward John Q. Adams Middle School. "The lake isn't really bottomless or water would be spilling out in China, and the descriptions of Trixie indicate a creature that is, quote, biologically unviable, unquote. But my nana is looking for a way to bring in a little extra cash at her souvenir shop. The Trixie eggs and the freeze-dried monster drool sell fine, but the Trixie-sighting maps are the biggest moneymaker she has. Guided Trixie tours are the next logical step." Agatha paused to pull in a gulp of air and slap a flyer on another telephone pole. "Plus Cousin Eleanor could use a job."

Cousin Eleanor was the black sheep of the humongous Wong family. Nana Wong was always complaining about the aggravation she caused.

"Not China," Orville managed to get in.

"What?" Agatha frowned at him.

"The water. It would be gushing out of Pakistan," Orville told her. "If the lake was bottomless."

Agatha gave a snort of laughter. "Pakistan? Really?" She shook her head. "Good thing my best friend is the original Encyclopedia Man, or I would never have known the real deal. Anyway, subject change. I can't talk geography before eight. What's the assignment for your social skills class this week?"

"Meet eye, say hi," Orville answered. "I'm supposed to look at people and say hello when I see them for the first time each day. It's stupid."

"It's not stupid to make an effort to fit into society, Orville," Agatha answered. "I do it. For example— sometimes when I wake up, I have no desire to brush my hair. But do I show up at school with bed head? No. I get myself into the bathroom and spend half an hour carefully constructing a very attractive, artistic version of bed head. I do it because that's what is expected of me as a very-soon-to-be teenager in our society. All the magazines say so. So don't complain about having to spend two seconds saying hi every day."

Agatha suddenly realized she was doing it again. Ranting. It was just that when things were important to her—like Orville realizing that it would be a good thing to fit in more—she talked . . . and talked . . . and talked. . . .

"Sorry," Agatha muttered, eyes on the ground. She hated to apologize, even to her best friend. She wished she could just rub his shoulder or maybe muss up his sandy hair, like she could with any other guy. But Orville was different. He *really* didn't like to be touched.

"Do people actually care if you say hi to them or not?" Orville asked. "Why does it matter?"

"Look, Orville. You're brilliant. Way more brilliant than most people. You must have noticed by now that people make no sense. Accept it. *Math* makes sense, statistics, facts—people don't."

As they turned up the walkway leading to the main entrance of the school, Agatha continued her pep talk. "I don't know why it matters that you say hi. And people probably don't give a whoop when you do. But if you *don't*, they might notice and think you're weird. And if people think you're weird, it's harder to get what you want. And what we BOTH want this year is to climb the John Q. Adams Middle School social ladder so that we're one tiny rung closer to popularity. Right?"

"I guess." Orville shrugged.

"I would suggest that you follow your social skills assignments without thought," Agatha told him. "That's the way the less brilliant of us do everything anyway. We think less and we're happier for it."

Agatha smiled at him, pushed open the half of the double door entrance that worked—only about half of *anything* at their school functioned—and led the way inside. Orville swung off toward his locker without bothering to say goodbye. Typical.

"Bye, Orville," Agatha called after him, doubting that he'd even hear. Orville spent a lot of time deep in his head, doing equations and other brainiac things she couldn't even begin to fathom.

That or he thought about airplanes, his one great love.

Agatha watched Orville retreat down the hall. *If only I could be Orville,* she thought. *Just for one day. Then I could get a peek at what goes on inside that amazing noggin—*

Her musings were interrupted by the smell of slightly sour milk.

Oh, well, she thought. *Time to get ready for class.* Agatha followed the curdled scent to her own locker, which was right next to the cafeteria.

"Abigail," a voice called. A guy voice.

Agatha turned around—and found Jack Simmons, every eighth-grade football-playing inch of him, standing there smiling at her. He was her crush. No, that was too ordinary, too bland. Jack was pretty much *every* seventh-grade girl's crush. But he was Agatha's *crunch*—and *he* wanted to talk to *her*.

For the first time in her life, Agatha had no idea what to say.

Suddenly Orville's voice came into her head. *Meet eye, say hi.* Agatha forced herself to look into Jack's dark blue eyes. "Hi," she managed to say.

"Abigail, hey," Jack said.

Agatha didn't bother to correct him. Jack Simmons was talking to her. That was enough. For now at least. She pushed a strand of thick dark hair behind her ear and hoped she didn't have food in her teeth.

"You know we have our big game against the Placid Sharks on Saturday," Jack continued.

"Yes, of course, uh-huh," Agatha answered. *One of those would have been fine*, she told herself. But now that she'd started talking, she couldn't stop. "Sharks versus the Sea Monsters. Big rivalry. Because we have to use their football field as our home field, since our school doesn't have a field. And they have that pro coach. And we have—"

Stop, Agatha ordered herself, clamping her teeth together. *He knows all this. What are you going to do next, give him a history of the sport?*

"Right," Jack said. Agatha felt her face flush as he

took a super-fast glance at his watch. "And so you know how the Monsters always do a prank on the Sharks the day of the game and they do one on us?"

"Yes," Agatha said. She snapped her teeth shut before she started babbling again.

"Well, I have a kickin' idea for our prank. Some friends and I made this big waterproof model of Trixie. We want to put it in the tank with the Placid shark," Jack explained.

"It's so wrong that their stupid shark pops up for every touchdown—even when we're using the field for *our* games," she jumped in. Agatha wanted Jack to know that even though she was just a seventh grader, she knew what was what. Besides, that metal shark and its big tank probably cost as much as it would for John Q. Adams to have its own football field and stands!

"Exactly!" Jack agreed. "That's why we want our prank to be an attack on the shark itself. We want our sea monster to rise out of the tank and spit fire at the shark during halftime."

"That would be so amazing!" Agatha exclaimed. She could picture it—Trixie blowing fire right into that obnoxious metal shark's open jaws.

"Yeah, but we can't figure out how to make Trixie move. Or, you know, breathe fire." Jack paused. "That kid you hang around with—he's a genius, right?"

Orville, Agatha realized. *He's only talking to me because I know Orville.*

She thought about that for a second and decided she didn't care. As long as Jack was speaking directly to her with what she called his "stun-a-bunny-with-beauty" smile, she was happy. "Oh, yeah. Orville could definitely figure out the mechanics," she assured him.

"Great. Can you two meet up with us at the shacks after school?"

The two of them. As in Agatha plus Orville. That might be tricky. Orville didn't like new people. Or unfamiliar situations.

"Definitely," Agatha told Jack. As if she could say anything else to her crunch.

"Cool. See you then."

Agatha's heart started doing a happy dance as soon as Jack ambled away. Hanging after school at the trailers John Q. used as extra classrooms wouldn't be a cause for joy to people who lived in, say, Paris, or L.A., or even Placid, Arizona. But it was It for Bottomless Lake—and Agatha had been invited.

Now all she had to do was get Orville there. No problem.

Or not a very big problem.

She hoped.

"Jack is popular. You hang around with Jack, *you* get to be popular. That's how it works," Agatha told Orville. "We could do a scientific study to prove it, but there's no time. For now, you're going to have to trust me. This is a golden opportunity, buddy. Golden."

Orville didn't take a step down the hallway that led toward the shacks. But he didn't make a move for the exit that would take him toward home either.

"Since the two of us met in second grade, we have been riding the broken-down bus to social anonymity," Agatha pressed her point. "This invitation is our boarding pass to the silver bird of ultra-popularity!"

Agatha stared at Orville. He blinked once. Twice.

Ugh! Agatha felt like pulling her hair out! As long as she and Orville had been friends, Orville had this annoying habit of not saying anything if he didn't think he had anything to say.

Nana Wong was always telling Agatha it was an annoying habit *she* should develop.

"Okay, let's back up," Agatha said. "Orville, do you think popularity is a good thing?"

"Define *good*," Orville answered.

My bad, she thought. *I've been talking to Orville as though he were me. As if what's important to me is important to him.* Orville was never going to care about being popular. It was time to try a different tactic.

"I can't believe I didn't even tell you what the prank is," Agatha said. "They want to put a model of Trixie in the tank behind the Sharks' goalposts. At halftime, the shark would pop up—you know, how it always does."

Orville nodded. Agatha knew it was his favorite part

of the football games she dragged him to. He loved picturing the machinery—the gears and levers and who knew what else—that made the shark leap from the water, then sink slowly down again.

"Well, this time Trixie would pop up too and shoot fire right into the shark's mouth!" Agatha rushed on.

"None of the sea monster lore mentions Trixie having fire-breathing abilities," Orville answered.

Agatha laughed. "Benjamin Orville Wright, I wish someday I could look inside your head, because I really don't understand you. You don't believe in Trixie. You tell every tourist who asks that Trixie couldn't possibly ever have existed. My grandmother has practically banned you from her souvenir shop because you are so bad for business. So if you don't believe in Trixie at all, why would you possibly care if, during the football prank, she breathes fire, or eats fire, or blows fire out her behind?"

Orville blinked. "I don't."

"So do you think you could do it?" Agatha asked. "Make Trixie pop up and figure out how to make the fire happen?"

Orville pulled a notebook out of his backpack, flipped it open, and started writing out a chemical equation.

In Orville world, that was a yes.

"I knew you wouldn't let me down!" Agatha cheered. "Follow me. We have a meeting to attend!"

She turned in the direction of the shacks and started walking. Orville shuffled along behind her.

He was still writing when they sat down at the splintery picnic table behind the trailers. Agatha placed herself directly across from Jack (!).

Lissa Roos—the eighth-grade class president—was there too. So was Jack's teammate, eighth grader Nathan Shoffer, and . . .

Stu Frysley?

Agatha frowned. Stu Frysley was in her homeroom class, but she'd never thought she'd share a picnic table with him, because she hated him with the fire of a thousand suns. She used to hate him with the fire of *ten* thousand suns. But five years of being best friends with Orville had mellowed her a little.

Orville didn't notice the majority of stuff that made Agatha go berserk—and by now Agatha had actually stopped noticing some of it too. But Stu was another story. There was no way she was ever going to hold hands with him and sing a chorus of "Give Peace a Chance." Hating him with the fire of a thousand suns was as low as she could go.

The only *good* thing she could say about Stu was that he was the reason she became friends with Orville in the first place. . . .

One day, way back in the second grade, Stu had gotten bored with picking his nose and had switched over to coming up with nicknames for Orville. Really creative gems like "Doo-doo Head" and "Retardo." Back then most people (even teachers) didn't understand that Orville had a condition called Asperger's syndrome—that while on the outside Orville wore a don't-knock-no-one's-home face, on the inside he had a Pentium 100 chip for a brain.

Agatha—who hated even the unfairness of the Trix rabbit never getting any cereal—really, *really* hated the way Stu Boogerman treated Orville. So one day before school, when Stu had hurled a particularly hurtful insult at Orville, Agatha threw her backpack at Stu's head.

It was the beginning of her war with Stu. And her friendship with Orville.

How Stu had made it to the top of the social food chain in middle school was a mystery to Agatha. Maybe it was just because his older brother, Brian, was cool. These things were hard to call. Agatha and Orville themselves were somewhere in the squishy middle—the lower squishy middle.

Well, it was better than the bottom, she guessed.

"Welcome to the prank planning committee," Lissa said, pulling Agatha out of her thoughts.

"I'm the secretary," Stu announced with an air of self-importance.

Agatha saw no need to respond to him. Neither did anyone else.

"So he's in?" Jack asked, jerking his chin toward Orville.

"Absolutely," Agatha answered. "He's working out the details right now."

The group watched in silence as Orville continued to scratch away in his notebook.

"Are you sure he's even doing anything real?" Stu asked, half under his breath. "I thought the guy was retarded."

Instantly Agatha was on her feet. She knew Orville hadn't heard Stu's comment. Orville was in the zone, and you could pretty much dance around naked in front of him when he was in the zone and he'd notice zippo.

But Agatha had heard Stu. And she wasn't having it. "What's wrong with you, Frysley? Haven't you been paying attention for the last five years? Orville isn't retarded. He's smarter than all of us put together. You look at him, and you think because his face doesn't have that much expression, or because he's a little clumsy, or because—"

"Hey, chill." Jack's hands were on Agatha's shoulders, guiding her back to her seat. She hardly felt them. "Stu's the one who's mentally damaged. We all know that."

"Yeah," Lissa agreed. "Orville's so smart he was placed in my eighth-grade advanced math class. I've seen him figure out a problem in three seconds."

Stu slapped his binder on the wooden table. "All I

know is that I'm supposed to be taking notes here. And I can't take notes if Mr. Wizard doesn't say anything."

Agatha glanced over at Orville. Yep, he was still in the zone. She reached over and plucked the pencil out of his hand, then covered his notebook with her own. "Do you think you could give us an update?" she asked. She shot Stu a meaningful look. "A *simple* one. So our secretary can keep up."

Orville looked like he was returning from a trip to the bottom of the ocean or some other galaxy. He blinked a few times, then nodded. "We'll make Trixie jump up using a remote-controlled lift under her feet."

"Cool," Nathan said. "What about the fire?"

"I'll put a container of dry sodium in Trixie's mouth, and a pump that will bring water up from the tank. The pump will be on the same remote. The water pressure will break the container of sodium." Orville nodded again.

Agatha didn't get it. She looked from face to face. Nobody else did either.

"And then what happens?" she asked.

"When dry sodium and water mix?" Orville asked.

"Yeah," the rest of them answered.

"You get fire," Orville explained. "I've calculated the correct amount of sodium to give just enough flame to last the fifteen seconds the shark is above the water."

"When the shark sinks, it will look like Trixie annihilated it!" Jack exclaimed. "Sweet!"

"And there's no danger that the fire could get out of control?" Lissa asked. "I think the prank's fantastic, but only if we can be completely sure nothing will go wrong."

"Orville is Mr. Safety," Agatha promised her. It was true, too. Orville had the town safety ordinances memorized, as well as the school rules, traffic codes, and laws that were so old they made you laugh—like the one that made it illegal to sing in a public place while wearing a swimsuit. Orville really liked rules, and no matter what, he always followed them.

"So we sneak into Placid tomorrow night and get Trixie set up in the tank, okay?" Jack announced.

Wow! Agatha thought. *A night hanging out with the popular kids. Trespassing and tinkering with Placid Middle School property. Could this be more amazing?*

For some reason, a shiver ran down her spine.

Orville noted that his heart rate had dropped. He estimated the drop rate to be roughly one and a half percent. That wasn't in the usual range for his visits to Placid—generally his heart rate dropped much lower than that. He decided he must be nervous, and therefore his heart was beating faster than usual.

A series of experiments several years ago had proved to Orville's satisfaction that it was the sharp angles of Placid—the perfect town square and the rectangular-shaped lawns—that caused the physical effect. The regularity of the shapes, the careful color schemes, and the organization of the street names combined to make Placid an extremely orderly place. Numbers in sequence for streets running north to south. Letters in sequence for streets running east to west. Orville calculated that his heart rate would drop between 0.2 and 0.3 percent more if the streets had just letters as their names. But at least the streets had names that *started* with the appropriate letter. Alphabet Soup Street, for example. Bouncing Baby Lane. Each street was named after one of the favorite things of Albert L. Placid—the billionaire who'd founded the town.

Yes, it was the orderliness of Placid that made his heart rate slow considerably when he was here. But not tonight. Tonight was different.

"Are you nervous?" Agatha whispered as they started across the thick grass of the Placid Middle School football field—Bermuda grass, but overseeded with perennial rye or it wouldn't be quite so lush, Orville decided.

"Yes," Orville answered. "What percentage is your heart rate up?"

"I don't know. A lot," Agatha said in a rush. "Do I look okay?" She stopped abruptly and turned to face him.

Orville stared at her. He didn't know what to say. Agatha looked like Agatha. Epicanthic fold in the eyelids and blue eyes—genetic contributions from her Chinese American father and her Irish American mother. Brown hair with some red strands in it. Sneaker laces tied in double knots. She smelled like Cocoa Puffs and starch.

"What? Am I hideous? Do I have a booger or something?" Agatha demanded, scrubbing at her nose.

"No. Your parents left for Russia tonight," Orville answered.

"Yeah. I'm not even going to ask how you knew that. They weren't supposed to leave until next week," Agatha told him. "And of course, Nana gave me Cocoa Puffs to cheer me up. I've hated Cocoa Puffs since third grade, ever since I had that weird nightmare about Sonny the Cuckoo Bird chasing me with a spoon. But Nana looks so happy when she sets that big bowl of chocolate gunk in front of me. How am I supposed to tell her?"

Agatha used a disproportionately greater number of words than Orville did. But he didn't mind. In fact, he liked it, although sometimes he used some of Agatha's talking time to work on calculations.

"Oh, look, Jack's already here." Agatha pointed to the field house next to the large (approximately two-and-a-half meters by one-and-a-quarter meters) tank that held the mechanical Placid shark. Orville noted that the field house was an exact replica of Placid Middle School, but on a 100-to-1 scale. He also noted that Jack *and* Lissa were waiting next to the field house. But Agatha didn't mention Lissa at all.

"Come on, let's run," Agatha urged. She flew across the field, graceful as a gazelle. Orville followed as closely as he could, the backpack full of supplies bouncing against his shoulder.

Agatha slid to a stop in front of Jack, Lissa, and the model of Trixie. Orville noted once again that his theory was correct. This was definitely not the model of a creature that was biologically viable. Orville stopped right behind Agatha. She looked Jack in the eye. "Hi," she said. And that was it. Orville tried to remember the last time Agatha had said one word and quit.

He was still flipping through his mental files on the subject when Stu and Nathan showed up. They'd agreed to come in pairs so they'd be harder to spot by Placid school security, a plan Orville approved of.

"So, Mr. Wee-zard, you ready to do your stuff?" Stu asked. "Or are we all out here for nothing?"

Orville noticed that Stu had a splash of ketchup on his earlobe. That was an unusual place for ketchup. He unzipped his backpack and pulled out the water pump. Jack flipped back Trixie's head, her ant-like antennae bouncing.

It had been so easy to picture the pump inside Trixie's hollow abdomen in his mind, but Orville's hands felt like two slabs of meat as he tried to wire his creation into place. No matter how hard he tried, he could never make his fingers work the way he wanted them to. Finally he got it. He took a deep breath, then pulled the container of sodium out of his backpack.

"Let me do it," Agatha volunteered. "The space behind the teeth isn't that big, and my hands are smaller than yours."

Sometimes it seemed like Agatha could read his mind. Orville knew he could always count on her. For the millionth time, he wished he knew when it was right to smile. If only he could show her how happy he was to be her friend.

Orville remembered some studies he had read about ESP. It might be interesting to do a study with Agatha and himself. They'd need a control group, of course. . . .

"Got it," Agatha announced, pulling Orville away from his thoughts. Once the pump was in place and the lift had been installed, Lissa and Nathan, the two tallest kids, hoisted Trixie into the tank. They worked the model into position directly opposite the metal shark.

"Can we see how it works?" Jack asked. "Not the fire. I know that's a one-shot thing. But Trixie coming out of—"

"Oh, no! There's someone on the field!" Lissa whispered.

"Security. We're doomed," Stu said, without bothering to lower his voice.

Nathan wrapped his hand over Stu's mouth.

"If the guard sees us by the tank, that's it. He'll

search it and find Trixie," Jack whispered. "Our prank will be ruined!"

Orville glanced over at Agatha. He always looked to Agatha when he wasn't sure what to do. This time, Agatha wasn't there.

Stu jerked his head to the side, breaking free of Nathan's grip. "I see your girlfriend bolted," he said to Orville. "Very nice."

A clatter rang out on the metal bleachers. Agatha! A flashlight beam caught her as she clambered down from the top, making more noise than should have been possible for someone of her weight. She must have shinnied up the side, Orville decided.

"Stop right there!" the security guard yelled.

But Agatha hit the ground running, jetting away from the tank, away from Orville and the others.

"I'm going after them," Jack said.

"Don't," Orville ordered. "She wants us to get away."

"She's sacrificing herself for the team," Nathan agreed. "That's really cool of her."

"I don't want her to get in trouble," Lissa worried.

Orville did a fast calculation. "She won't. She can outrun the security guard."

They all stared at him.

"Agatha is aerodynamic," he explained.

Chapter 2

"Any second I'm going to float away. That's how happy I am," Agatha told Orville as they headed for A Monster's Paradise, her grandmother's souvenir shop. "But don't let me, okay? I don't want to miss one second of my über-popularity. I mean, *ours*. In less than two hours, we're going to be sitting with Lissa Roos and her friends at the biggest football game of the year! Plus Stu, but whatever, because after the game we're hanging out with Jack. And Nathan too!"

"The force of gravity equals the universal gravitational constant times the two masses in question—in this case, you and the earth—divided by the distance between the two masses squared," Orville said. "And I didn't add in the weight of the cookies."

"As I often must, I ask, 'Huh?'" Agatha answered.

"Although you weigh less than the average for girls your height, there is no possibility that you will float away," Orville explained. "As the equation illustrates."

"Oh, right. Cookies, please." Concentrating hard, Orville managed to balance the boxes of Trixie-head cookies he'd been carrying on top of the ones Agatha held in her arms. "I'll try not to stay in there long. But you know Nana. Oh, and remember not to talk to any tourists who are on their way into the shop unless you want to see Nan's toad-who-ate-a-snake face."

Orville nodded, and Agatha backed into the shop so she wouldn't crush the cookie boxes. The smell of A Monster's Paradise hit her first—incense, leather, plastic, algae, and Nana's Windsong perfume. The sounds came right on top of the scent: bubbles from the aquarium filter, "The Ballad of Bottomless Lake" playing on the ancient record player, Nana gossiping with whichever relative happened to be in the store that day, the tinkle of the three bells hanging from the door.

"Where do you want these?" Agatha asked. She turned around, and the glitter-o-rama that was the shop dazzled her eyes. Sparkling Trixie mobiles hung from the ceiling, pyramids of fuchsia Trixie eggs brightened the back corner, and aquariums filled with turquoise blue water dotted the display shelves.

Agatha smiled at her auntie Louise, who was manning the main counter. Auntie Louise gave a little wave.

Louise was Agatha's great-aunt—one of three great-aunts and two great-uncles on Nana Wong's side. Aside from all the "great" relatives, Agatha had thirteen *regular* aunts and uncles and, at last count, about thirty cousins. Orville told Agatha that when you counted up all of Agatha's aunts, uncles, and cousins combined, the

Wong family made up nearly five percent of the population of Bottomless Lake.

It made family gatherings *very* interesting.

"How many did he send?" Nana Wong's voice asked, although Agatha couldn't spot her nana among all the clutter. The effect was kind of spooky.

"Four boxes," Agatha answered. "The big ones."

Nana sighed. "Why does your uncle keep making them?"

"Why do you keep buying them?" Agatha countered.

One of the big Trixies began moving toward Agatha, its giant purple-and-silver feet slapping on the polished wood floor. It took Agatha a second to realize that the creature had her grandmother's head.

"Just wait until you have children of your own," Nana said. She pointed to the massive pirate chest in the front window. Agatha stuck the boxes of cookies her uncle Jim had made inside.

"So if, *if* I have children of my own, I'm expected to buy whatever horrid inedible things they make?" Agatha asked.

"Yes. If you own a shop where it's appropriate that such things be sold," her grandmother answered.

"But the heads, they don't look like Trixie heads," Agatha argued. "They look like mushrooms. And I'm being kind."

"Unzip, please," Nana Wong said, turning Trixie's tail

toward Agatha. She waved her hand toward a zipper running underneath the monster's scales. "A, um, plus-size customer wanted to know if this would fit, and now I can tell her it will." Agatha's grandmother gave a relieved sigh as Agatha released her from the plastic suit. "Oh, and sweetie, we have the baby cousins overnight tonight."

"Great," Agatha grumbled. It seemed to her that at any given moment, at least one of her cousins was underfoot—meddling, snooping, getting in the way, or, in the babies' case, making foul smells.

The only Wong family members who *weren't* constantly around were Agatha's parents. They were always flying off to someplace or other. It had something to do with their jobs.

Agatha wondered what kind of job required her parents to fly to Russia and Uzbekistan and Sri Lanka. Then she thought that knowing her parents, it was most likely something *extremely* boring.

"If—again I say *if*—I have children, I'm definitely not going to allow them to live in the same town as I do after they grow up," Agatha announced. "We have way, way too many relatives around here." She leaned in to kiss Nana goodbye. "And if you feed the babies anything stinky, *you* have to change them."

Agatha turned and headed for the door.

She smiled when she saw Orville waiting for her outside. Her family might be totally insane, but when she was with Orville . . . it was like stepping into a bubble of calm. Maybe she wasn't calm, exactly. But any crisis that came up came from her. And if you asked him something, Orville would be ready with an answer.

"Ready to go, go, Monsters?" Agatha asked.

Orville blinked.

Agatha rephrased. "Ready to go to the game?"

"Yes," Orville said. "Let's go."

"You guys, over here!" Lissa called as Agatha led Orville toward the Albert L. Placid snack stand next to the Albert L. Placid Middle School parking lot. Lissa had saved them a place in the snack line. "I'm so excited about the game," she exclaimed. Then she lowered her black cat-eye glasses—the ones that made Agatha wish *she* had bad vision so *she* could have a pair—and gave a fast wink. "And the halftime show, of course!"

"If it actually works," Stu grumbled as he joined them. "I mean, look at who *made* it."

Agatha wished she could throw her backpack at his head the way she used to. But she'd vowed to give up physical violence—unless absolutely necessary—when she entered middle school. It didn't go with her new wardrobe.

"Want some mustard with that jealous, Stu?" Agatha asked super-politely. She studied the snack stand menu and tried to remind herself that a really good choke hold was so not the middle school Agatha.

"You want some mustard with that face, Agatha?" Stu asked. Violence was clearly still part of Stu's middle school repertoire. *The infant*, Agatha thought, ignoring him.

"What are you going to get, Orville?" Lissa asked.

"Brought mine," Orville answered. "Tuna with sea monster slime."

The same lunch Orville eats every day, Agatha thought with a smile. Sea monster slime was really just sweet pickle relish. But Bottomless Lake's stores—including Nana Wong's—sold the relish to the tourists as edible slime.

"Hey, I love that stuff," Lissa exclaimed. "Sea monster slime is like my favorite thing!"

Cool, Agatha thought. *Orville and the eighth-grade class president bonding! I knew there was something worthy about Lissa. And if she can get Orville to loosen up, we'll have a seat on that silver bird of popularity for sure!*

As Orville explained to Lissa the exact proportion of tuna to relish that he used in his sandwiches, something hard bumped against Agatha's shoulder. Agatha turned around and saw a guy with way too much hair product holding a large video camera—like the ones you saw on the news. "Sorry," he told her.

"He's a klutz," a tall red-haired girl holding a microphone added. She gave hair-product guy an affectionate pat on the shoulder. "We're here to do a little piece about the game." She looked Agatha up and down, then turned toward Lissa. "I'm Samantha Boutry. I cover sports for the Sharks TV station."

TV station? Agatha's mind whirled as it attempted to process this information. John Q. Middle School's AV department consisted of one slightly broken slide projector—and the Placid kids had a whole *TV station?* The unfairness of it totally boggled the mind.

"You don't mind if I step in front of you, do you?" Samantha asked Agatha.

Agatha couldn't make her mouth form words— which was happening to her more and more often lately. She just nodded.

Samantha stepped up to the snack counter and ran a brush through her hair. Then she frowned at her hand— the one holding the mike—and ran a nail file over one minutely ragged nail. She handed the brush and file to her cameraman, who jammed them in his pocket, their brightly colored handles sticking strangely out of his jeans.

"Sam Boutry for Shark TV here." She smiled directly into the camera. "I'm picking up my munchies before the big game!" She looked over her shoulder at the freckle-faced girl behind the counter. "What's selling the best today?" she asked.

"Is that how you decide what you want?" Stu called out. "By what's the most popular?"

Samantha's smile vanished. She made a "cut" motion

across her throat. "Great. Now I'm going to have to start again."

"Don't you know how television works over at your school?" the camera guy demanded.

"Yeah, what's your damage, Frysley?" a boy near Agatha called. She didn't need to look over to know who he was. The smell was enough. She glanced to the left to confirm it. Yep, Richie Cruz. He used to be on her cousin Billy's Little League soccer team. And even back then, he'd worn aftershave. Way, way, *way* too much aftershave. He didn't shave, of course. He didn't need to. Agatha wondered if he truly understood the concept of *after*shave.

"He's from Bottomless Lake. Does that answer your question?" scoffed a girl with dark hair twisted into a dozen mini-buns.

"Think you can say that again with a mouthful of dirt?" Stu asked Richie, ignoring the girl.

For a second, Agatha wondered if she'd made Stu afraid of girls during all their elementary school tussles.

"Stu, to the bleachers—now," Lissa ordered, stepping between the boys.

"But I want a cheeseburger," Stu whined.

"I'll get it," Lissa shot back. She turned to Agatha. "You and Orville get him out of here. What do you want?"

"Hot dog and an orange soda," Agatha answered. She

grabbed Stu by the arm, her grip just a little tighter than it needed to be. She pulled him out of the snack stand and marched him over to the front row of the Monsters' bleachers—perfect for Jack-viewing—and sat him down. She and Orville took seats next to him.

"Are you going to be a good boy now?" Agatha asked Stu, using the same voice she reserved for Auntie Louise's ugly little dog, Miss Bon Bon.

Stu just snorted in reply.

"I'm so ready to scream my lungs out for Ja—I mean, for the Monsters," Agatha announced. She turned to Orville with a grin. "And yes, I know that's not physically possible. I just mean I'm going to yell really loud."

Cheering for Jack, she could do. Talking to him . . . that was still kind of hard. But after the game, it would be easy to come up with things to say. Like, "We wouldn't have won it without you, Jack." Or she could compliment him on a specific play.

Agatha knew football. She and her multitudinous cousins played touch—well, knock-you-down touch—at every family get-together. Yeah, she'd keep her eye out for Jack's best play and casually mention it when the prank committee got together to celebrate their victory.

Agatha shot a glance at Orville. He was calmly eating one triangle of his tuna-and-sea-monster-slime sand-wich. He ate it so that it retained its triangle shape until the very last bite. *What would it be like not to worry about what to say or what people think about you?* she wondered. For the millionth time, she wished she could be just a little more like Orville.

She knew you had to care to some degree. She totally meant it when she nagged Orville to do his assignments for the social skills class his parents made him take. But caring too much was likely a problem too. When had she started caring so much? She didn't used to. Had she crossed the line? Was she—?

"The princess is back," Stu announced. Agatha followed his gaze to the entrance of the Monsters' bleachers. Samantha Boutry was interviewing John Q. students, her cameraman right behind her. Agatha couldn't hear what Samantha was asking the students, but she couldn't help noticing that Samantha was only talking to the kids with the best hair and the best clothes. She also noticed that Ms. Winogrand, the purple-haired John Q. art teacher, kept trying, and failing, to get on camera.

"Why doesn't Samantha go over to her own side?" Stu muttered.

"What is your deal?" Agatha asked him. "You're being more bellicose than usual today."

Stu's mouth worked, but no sounds came out. Agatha smiled. She enjoyed using words that Stu didn't understand. Of course, she'd only learned that *bellicose* meant "warlike" the day before yesterday—when Nana asked her to help Cousin Serena study for her SATs—but Stu didn't know that.

"I believe madame had the bowwow de hot and the eau de orange," Lissa called as she climbed over the nearby students to reach Agatha, Orville, and Stu. She handed Agatha her food and a large soda, then tossed a foil-wrapped burger at Stu. "Scooch," she told him, and when Stu slid down the bleacher, Lissa plopped down between him and Agatha.

This is so almighty cool—I'm sitting next to the most popular girl in school, Agatha thought.

"Do you guys know Edmundo and Kit?" Lissa asked. Without waiting for an answer, she went on. "Edmundo and Kit, meet Agatha and Orville." Kit and Edmundo took seats on the bleachers. Orville remembered to do his meet eye–say hi thing. Agatha smiled and gave a little wave that she hoped looked cute.

The Placid cheerleaders began stretching in the end zone.

"It's so weird to see Tina Gore in a Shark cheerleading outfit," Edmundo commented, glancing down at the field.

"If I was her, I would love to cheer against the John Q. Monsters, because then I'd be cheering against Matthew Lopez," Kit chimed in.

"You know about this, right?" Lissa asked Agatha.

"Matthew asked Tina to the Enchanted Lake Dance last year. She was so psyched—bought a new dress and all that. Then Matthew canceled at the last minute because Coach Pettit said he needed to spend the night doing drills to improve his football game."

Agatha gasped with what she hoped was the right amount of horror. "Whoa. What a jerk!"

"Seriously," Lissa agreed.

"Why is it weird to see Tina Gore in a Shark cheer-leading outfit?" Orville asked.

"Tina used to be a Monster cheerleader," Agatha explained, happy that Orville was trying to follow along with the conversation. "She transferred to Placid when her mom got a job with the Alfred L. Placid software company."

"Everyone in this town works for Alfred L. some-how," Edmundo added. "It's kind of creepy. Big Brother and all that."

"Just like we all serve the sea monster," Lissa joked.

It was true, Agatha realized. Nana Wong sold souvenirs. Lissa's dad owned The Grotto, an underwater restaurant, where tourists dined while looking directly into the depths of the lake, hoping for a glimpse of Trixie. And Orville's father trained the swimming pigs for the underwater show at The Grotto. (He had explained once that people got so distracted by the swimming pigs, they tended to forget they hadn't seen a sea monster.)

"Sorry to interrupt, but I was wondering if I could get your opinion on the new Shark uniforms?" Samantha Boutry had reappeared, mike in hand, cameraman in tow.

Lissa shot a warning look at Stu. "Well, they're nice and everything," she answered politely. "But kind of unoriginal. The Monsters have always had green with red letters as *our* colors. Why did you guys switch to red with green this year?"

Agatha grinned. Lissa was being perfectly nice, but she'd still managed to get in a dig at the Sharks.

"We triumphed over them last season," a guy behind Agatha called out. "Maybe they're hoping some of our luck will rub off on them if they steal our colors." Everyone in Agatha's section laughed. The Monster cheerleaders immediately got in on the action. They spun toward the Shark bleachers and began to chant:

> *Our team is red hot!*
> *Your team is all shot!*
> *Our team is*
> *R-E-D!*
> *H-O-T!*
> *Red hot!*

Agatha punched her fist in the air, yelling and leaping up and down.

A moment later, the Shark cheerleaders shot back a cheer from the end zone:

That's all right
That's okay
You're gonna pump our gas someday!

A kid in a shark mascot costume shook his butt in the direction of the John Q. fans. Agatha booed along with the other kids from John Q.

Orville turned to Agatha. "I don't understand that cheer. What does it have to do with football?" he asked.

"Nothing," Kit burst out. "It was just mean."

"Kit's right," Agatha added. "Everyone at Placid is rich, so they think that makes them better and smarter than everyone at John Q. They think that all we're capable of is pumping gas or asking, "Do you want fries with that?" What jerks. I'd put your brain up against anybody's in Placid—adults included."

"I still don't understand why they're cheering about something that doesn't have to do with football," Orville repeated.

"Sometimes these things don't make sense to me either," Agatha answered, staring across the field at the Placid cheerleaders.

Agatha loved her school. She loved her town. Mostly she didn't care that the Placid kids had so much more of . . . everything. So why did they have to waste time cheering about it?

"Hey, I see our guys lining up!" Lissa exclaimed. She pointed over to the door of the Placid locker rooms.

The Monster cheerleaders trotted over and two of them unrolled a large paper banner with SEA MONSTERS spelled out in big sparkly letters. They positioned the banner over the locker room door and shouted out Sean Fuller's name as he came bursting through the paper. Two more cheerleaders instantly got another banner in place for the next player to crash through.

Jack ran out last of all. Agatha actually felt something pop in her throat as she shouted for him. She swallowed some of her orange soda and tried to pace herself. She needed to save some larynx for the killer plays she knew Jack was going to make—the ones she was going to chat with him about post-game.

Except he didn't make great plays. At least not in the first quarter. He only made plays he'd want to forget. Plays *everyone* at John Q. would want to forget. He even handed off the ball to someone on the Shark team!

The kid in the shark mascot costume did a cartwheel

At the start of the second quarter, Jack made a beautiful pass. Agatha's stomach soared with the ball, flying in the air. Then it thudded down when the ball landed solidly in the hands of one of the Sharks—as if Jack had been aiming at the guy all along!

"Jack Simmons seems to want to transfer to Placid," Samantha Boutry commented from the sportscaster's booth over by the Shark bleachers. "We'll see how you do in the second half, Jack! Get us a few more points and it's a done deal!"

Agatha let out a moan. "What is wrong with him today?"

"I don't know. Depending on whether or not Jack is left- or right-handed, there should be a connection between the gyroscopic and aerodynamic torques that would result in a slight curve to the right or left," Orville commented. "But only slight. It wouldn't explain a variation to the degree we just saw."

Agatha was too depressed to ask for a translation into English.

Jack's playing got worse and worse as the quarter wore on. When the refs' whistles blew, signaling the end of the first half, Agatha felt relieved. She didn't want to have to watch anymore.

The Monsters were down by twenty-one points. Twenty-one. Agatha felt like she'd eaten twenty-one ice cubes. Or like she had twenty-one boulders on her head. Or twenty-one worms in each of her shoes.

She could only imagine how Jack felt. What was wrong with him?

Orville's gaze returned to Edmundo's sneaker. The plastic tab at the end of one of his very white shoelaces was missing. Maybe broken off in the washing machine. Would the motion of the machine be likely to chip a piece of the tab free? The variety of washer was key. And the cycle—

"Stay with me, Orville," Agatha whispered. "The Shark cheerleaders just finished their routine. We're getting close to liftoff."

Liftoff? Orville thought. There was nothing he would rather think, talk, or dream about than flying. Planes, rockets, space shuttles, even hang gliders—these were his favorite subjects in the world.

"Not liftoff," Agatha quickly corrected herself. "You know. Time for you to work your magic. Not magic. I know it's not magic. I'm talking about go time."

He processed that string of Agatha-isms and realized that she was talking about the Trixie prank. "Okay," Orville told her. He slid the small remote out of his backpack and cupped it in his hand.

"Please welcome the Monster marching band with their rendition of our state song, 'Arizona'!" Samantha Boutry said from the sports box.

"You're not going to let this distract you, right?" Agatha asked. She got her face so close to his that Orville could smell her strawberry lip gloss. (He knew it was strawberry because Agatha had told him. It didn't smell like strawberries. It was more like strawberry Jell-O.) He pulled back from her. She almost never violated the no-touching zone, but she'd just gotten kind of close. This no-distractions thing must be important to her.

Orville wished he didn't have a no-touching zone. He'd observed that Agatha showed affection through physical contact. Hugging, playfully punching, hair smoothing, shoulder bumping . . .

Orville had a long list of Agatha contacts, and he had frequently seen her deliver them to her many family members. He knew it was typical Agatha behavior with people she cared about. But he could never make himself comfortable with it. Even his parents had to respect the no-touching zone. The doctor said it was normal for someone with his condition, but Orville wished he could get over it anyway.

"I need you to concentrate. I know the part in the song about 'the sun flaming' makes you crazy because a flaming sun would be a very, very bad thing, but—" Agatha stopped as a commotion broke out in the Monster stands.

"Booo!" a ponytailed girl across the aisle shouted.

Next to her, a freckle-faced girl laughed loudly. "Wow! That's the worst job they've ever done!"

Orville tried to calculate what the uproar was about. The band sounded the same as usual—some flat notes, some sharp, but some on key. "Arizona" was a stupid song, but no one had ever minded that before. About sixty percent of the Monster fans were jeering, while the remaining forty percent were booing. Was booing and laughing at your own school's band normal? He would have to ask his social skills teacher, Miss Eloise.

Now most people in the Shark bleachers were cheering. Why would they cheer for something that the Monsters laughed and booed at?

Then Orville saw them—the big shark bite marks streaked with blood painted down the backs of the Monster band's uniforms.

With embarrassment, Orville realized that everyone else had noticed the shark bites right away. He didn't always focus on the same details as other people.

"*That's* Placid's prank?" Stu demanded between fits of giggles. "It *bites*. You get it? Bites."

"That's a really lame prank." Lissa chuckled.

"It's pathetic," Agatha agreed. "It's like they didn't even try."

"We're competing with a bunch of senile Depends wearers!" Stu laughed even harder.

"Oh, very nice, Stu," Lissa said. She twisted her silver pinky ring around her finger. Orville noticed that it left a green streak on her skin.

"Come on," Stu complained, his voice rising several decibels. "Are you telling me that isn't a totally poor prank? It isn't even low-tech. It's no-tech."

"The Sharks fans are cheering," Orville pointed out. "They seem to like the prank."

"Listen to them, Orville," Agatha said. "They're not putting any feeling into it. They're nowhere near as loud as they should be. They all know their prank is dumb."

"They did get Brad Purcell to have a hissy fit right on the field," Kit noted. "Check it out, he just smashed through his bass drum."

"No biggie. Brad has anger management issues," Lissa informed the group. "That's his third drum this season."

"Even *with* the hissy fit, our prank is so much more fabulous than Placid's. In fact, this may be the best prank in the history of our school!" Agatha smiled proudly at Orville.

Orville wished one more time that what he felt on the inside just automatically twitched his face into an expression that anyone could read. Then Agatha could look at him and know that just sitting next to her on the bleachers made him feel happy.

But his face didn't have a lot of expression. It was just part of who he was. His brain, though, that worked fine. Orville did a quick compare and contrast of every element of their upcoming prank versus the Sharks' prank—from the technical expertise required, to the shock value, to the amusement factor—and their prank came out on top all the way.

"I agree with you," he told his best friend. "Our prank is better. One hundred percent."

The band finished up "Arizona" and marched off the field to the Monster fight song. Brad yanked off his drum and kicked it. Orville didn't know why he was so upset. The red paint on the band's uniforms was already running. It was likely that the perpetrator had used the water-soluble kind.

In its tank behind the opposite goalpost, the metal Placid Shark reared up. A roar of victory—a sound no actual shark had the physiology to make—ripped out over the loudspeakers.

"Now, Orville!" Agatha urged.

Orville pushed the blue button on his remote, keeping his eyes glued to the shark tank. Immediately Trixie rose out of the deep blue water of the tank. She faced the shark, her mouth open, fangs dripping very realistic plaster foam.

Orville pushed the red button. He imagined the water from the tank pumping up through Trixie's body, breaking the tube of sodium, and . . .

WHOOOSH! Fire burst out of Trixie's mouth, shooting straight at the roaring shark.

There was an inrush of air, as if everyone in the stadium had gasped at once (although that was statistically unlikely). Then everyone in the Monster bleachers started hooting and clapping and even dancing, while everyone in the Shark bleachers broke out in boos.

The shark sank back into the water. "Trixie killed it!" Stu shouted.

Kit picked up the chant. "Trixie killed the shark! Trixie killed the shark!"

Agatha joined in. And Lissa. And Edmundo. And the girl sitting behind Orville, the one with braces who had been eating popcorn.

Then Orville felt the words coming out of his own mouth. "Trixie killed the shark! Trixie killed the shark!"

It felt strange to be so in sync with a group, Orville thought. But it was *good* strange. He yelled even louder.

Then Agatha screamed. She grabbed his arm. She never grabbed him—it was the ultimate no-touching-zone violation. As Orville pulled himself away, Agatha pointed to the field house next to the tank. Through the windows, he could see orange flames. They filled the building.

BAM! BAM! Two of the field house windows blew out.

More oxygen, Orville thought. *The key element a fire needs to keep burning*. In an instant, the flames were consuming the field house walls and roof.

Beside Agatha, Lissa let out a shriek. Now the flames were racing along the grass—following the white chalk lines that marked out the yards on the playing field!

The cheerleaders squealed and ran from the field.

The Shark football players took off right after them. The kid in the shark mascot costume seemed confused by all the yelling. He tried to run, but his costume tripped him up. He fell to the grass. Luckily, two John Q. players grabbed him under the arms and dragged him away from the flames.

Smells Orville recognized from chemistry class singed his nose—sulfur, magnesium, copper. Smoke began to burn his eyes.

"Keep calm, everyone," a Placid teacher called from the sports box. "Exit the bleachers row by row, starting from the bottom. Then make your way calmly to the back of the parking lot."

"You heard what he said," called Mr. Pettit, John Q.'s football coach, as he trotted over to the Monster bleachers. He had his windbreaker zipped up to his nose. "I want to see this row moving and no one else." He pointed to Agatha and Orville's row. "Go! Go! Go!"

Orville slipped out of his seat and hurried away from the bleachers.

"Ugh! It smells like rotten eggs," Kit complained as they made their way to the exit.

"More like cow poop," Stu added.

"Ohhh, it's terrible!" Edmundo moaned, retching as he walked through the aisle.

Agatha held her nose and made her way out of the stadium. She didn't say a word until they had reached the back of the parking lot. "Orville," she whispered. "Trixie's flames were aimed toward that field house." He noticed that her pupils were wide. "Could *we* have started that fire?"

Lissa stepped up next to her. "Hey! I thought you said our prank was safe," she cried.

"Orville, tell me," Agatha said again. "Did *we* do that?"

Chapter 3

"Agatha Wong," Ms. Dooly called in her soft voice, which for some reason reminded Agatha of baby powder.

Before Agatha could utter the word "here," a metallic squeal came over the PA system and another voice called her name. "Agatha Wong. Orville Wright. To Principal Rothman's office immediately."

There was the usual soft *oooh.* You couldn't get called to the principal's office without it. Ms. Dooly scrunched her face into a sad, surprised look Agatha labeled "kitten-splashed-with-water" and waved Agatha toward the door.

Moving on autopilot, Agatha made her way out into the hallway with a normal expression on her face. But the second she was alone—total freakage. She was sure she was wearing her ate-a-whole-jalapeño-in-one-bite look.

"It's the fire. We're getting blamed for the fire," she muttered, talking to herself like a crazy person. "But Orville said it wasn't our fault," she continued, forcing her feet to walk the speckled linoleum toward the principal's office. "He said it was impossible. And if Orville said it, it has to be true."

Agatha turned the corner and saw the person she

most wanted to see shuffling toward her from the opposite direction—Orville. He was wearing his Monday outfit, just as he did every week. He would have had a closet full of the exact same clothes—just like Einstein did—if Agatha hadn't intervened when they started middle school. They had compromised on seven outfits, one for each day.

Right now, Agatha couldn't help but love the sameness of Orville—his steadiness—his dependability.

Yes, you can count on B. Orville Wright, Agatha thought. *Even when you're staring in the face of certain doom—the principal's office.*

Agatha reached the door of the office first. She was too nervous to walk slowly. When Orville reached her, he looked her in the eye. "Hi," he said.

The one word squeezed at her heart. "Hi, Orville," Agatha choked out. She opened the door and led the way inside. Mr. Ben, the school secretary, pointed to Principal Rothman's open door. He wasn't smiling. Agatha didn't think she'd *ever* seen Mr. Ben without a smile before. Orville would know for sure.

"Take a seat," Principal Rothman said when Agatha and Orville entered his office.

Agatha glanced around. *Yikes!* she thought. *It looks like Trixie threw up in here.*

There were a Trixie coffee mug, Trixie pencils, Trixie banners. Principal Rothman was even wearing a

Trixie baseball cap—complete with bouncing yellow antennae. He was obviously Mr. School Spirit. *Could that mean he liked the prank just a little teeny bit?* Agatha wondered.

You're deranged, you've lost it, you're cuckoo for Cocoa Puffs, she thought, answering her own question. She lowered herself onto the long green sofa across from the principal's desk. Orville sat down next to her. The principal gave them the stare-'n'-silence—the look designed to make you confess all.

Agatha wanted to grab the nearest throw pillow— embroidered with Trixie's face, of course—and cuddle it for comfort. But she didn't let herself. Show no weakness, that was her motto.

But why was she so nervous? It wasn't as if she'd never been in a principal's office before. Not since her backpack-flinging days, of course. (You couldn't fight for what was right and not face The Man once in a while.)

But the field house burned to the ground? The scorched football field? That was . . . monumental. Criminal, even.

The stare-'n'-silence continued. The Trixie clock on the wall ticked as the seconds crawled by.

At least she wasn't alone in here. Agatha knew Orville wouldn't break down. Silence didn't bother him. *Show no weakness,* she reminded herself, and stared right back at the principal, trying not to blink.

"I assume you know why you're here," Principal Rothman finally said.

"No," Orville answered.

Agatha shook her head. Of course she knew, but admitting to something you hadn't been accused of was never a good idea. Once in the fourth grade, she'd confessed to giving Stu a bloody nose when she'd really been called into the principal's office to get an award for a speech she'd written about the need for peace in the Middle East.

"Well, then, I assume you know about the fire that started during the Monster-Shark game on Saturday," Principal Rothman continued. "A fire that immediately followed our school prank—a prank that involved shooting flames."

"Yes," Orville and Agatha answered together.

Agatha really wanted that throw pillow now. She really, really did. She allowed herself to reach out and give it a quick stroke. Then she glanced at her best friend. He looked the same as ever. That helped too.

"After the fire, a few of us examined the John Q. halftime prank quite carefully," Principal Rothman explained. "We found the pump system inside the Trixie dummy, and I showed it to Mrs. Barba, our science expert. She noticed the trace of sodium. . . ."

He let the word hang in the air. Agatha tried to make her face as blank as Orville's, but she didn't think she succeeded very well.

Principal Rothman sighed. "Orville, we're all aware of how gifted you are, particularly in the sciences. Mrs. Barba and I agree that you're the only one in our school with the sophistication to come up with this sort of device."

The principal slid his gaze to Agatha. "And I have noticed that wherever Orville goes, you go too, Miss Wong."

It was actually the other way around, but Agatha didn't say that. She shot another glance at Orville. Principal Rothman hadn't asked Orville a direct question yet. That was good. Agatha knew that she had to be the one to do the talking.

She and Orville had been snagged. But no one else needed to get in trouble. She didn't want the rest of the prank committee brought into this. It could end right here—with the two of them.

"Of course, I had to inform the principal of Placid Middle School of our findings," Principal Rothman continued. "I had to tell her that students from my school were responsible for the fire. Neither school will be able to use the field this year—it can't be reseeded until spring. But due to the circumstances, John Q.'s rights to use the Placid field have been revoked. For *all* our teams. Permanently."

The room began to spin around Agatha—all the Trixies whirling past her. None of the John Q. sports teams would be able to play *ever again!* And Principal Rothman thought it was because of her and Orville!

Don't lose it now, Agatha ordered herself. *Don't you dare.* She tried to focus on Orville.

"If you and Mrs. Barba know Orville's work well enough to know he made the pump, you should also know that Orville doesn't make mistakes with measurements or calculations," Agatha told the principal, ignoring her dizziness. "We're not denying that we pulled the prank. But we are absolutely denying that our prank started the fire. Orville's incapable of messing up like that. His brain just doesn't work that way!"

Principal Rothman shook his head, his Trixie antennae waving back and forth. "Kids, I don't think you set the fire on purpose. But your prank sent flames flying in the direction of the field house. The field house went up moments later. Clearly a spark from your fire ignited some of the gardening chemicals in the field house."

"No," Orville said. "The field house fire was a separate occurrence."

It was the first thing he'd said, and it was a doozie. Agatha stared at him in shock. A separate fire? He'd never mentioned that before.

"It started 5.3 seconds after our prank ended. No spark from Trixie's mouth could have reached the field house—I did calculations and trials. But if a spark *had* hit flammable chemicals, they would have ignited immediately. There would not have been a 5.3-second delay," he concluded, his voice calm and even.

"Five point-three seconds? How could you come up with a number like that?" the principal asked doubtfully.

"Orville has an insanely accurate . . . whatchamacallit. Internal clock," Agatha jumped in. "Seriously. He knows these things."

Principal Rothman shook his head again. "Well, Orville's clock is off this time. There's no way that the field house fire coincidentally started right after your prank came to a close. Your prank started the fire—end of discussion. Now, I want you to give me the names of the other kids involved."

"No one! There was no one else," Agatha blurted as Orville started to open his mouth. She had to keep him quiet. He couldn't lie. His brain wasn't wired that way— lying wasn't logical. Or necessary. Or something.

Fortunately, Agatha was a first-class fibber. "It was just me and Orville," she stated. "We planned the whole prank. He's the brain. I'm the brawn." She flexed an arm muscle to support her statement.

The principal raised his eyebrow, taking in her four- foot-nine-inch height and eighty-eight-pound-soaking- wet-with-lots-of-shampoo-in-her-hair frame. "We can sit here all day," he said, unconvinced.

"Orville and I have a French test next period that we wouldn't mind missing," she bluffed, figuring he wouldn't know that she and Orville weren't in the same class.

"I don't take French," Orville told her, as if she didn't already know.

Agatha stared at her best friend. *Why can't he at least let me lie for him?* she silently wailed. But it was too late. They were caught. Principal Rothman was practically smirking.

"Why don't you wait in the outer office, Agatha?" he said. "I'd like to talk to Orville alone for a few minutes." The principal smiled as he walked to the door and opened it.

Agatha was out of options. They were doomed! Orville would tell him every single person involved in planning the prank. He would be a snitch—and he wouldn't even understand why that was bad.

She shuffled through the door and slumped down on the hard wooden bench. Less than fifteen seconds later, the PA system came to life with its usual ear-rending squawk. "Will Lissa Roos, Nathan Shoffer, Stu Frysley, and—"

Don't say it, don't say it, don't say it, Agatha silently begged.

"—Jack Simmons please come to the principal's office. Immediately."

Bam! Just like that, she and Orville were booted off the sweet silver bird of popularity.

She could already hear the life-as-a-loser-bus rattling toward her. No air-conditioning. No warm cookies. No free movies.

There would be no Jack. No Lissa. No cool clique to

hang out with—not after they realized that Orville had sold them out.

Agatha and Orville would be social outcasts . . . forever.

Twenty minutes later, after one long lecture about playing with fire and a sentence of one month's detention for all involved, the prank committee stood alone in the hall outside the principal's office.

"Thanks for ratting on us," Stu exploded. "What, you wouldn't have been happy without some company in detention?"

"No more football," Nathan mumbled, his eyes glazed. "Not this season, not *ever*."

"You guys swore the prank was safe," Lissa said, a sheen of tears covering her eyes. "I had this horrible nightmare last night that someone got killed in the fire. We could have killed someone!"

"No more football," Nathan repeated.

"You mean, *Orville* could have killed someone. He designed the thing," Stu corrected her.

"Why *did* you rat us out?" Nathan asked. "What was the point? We wouldn't have done it to you." He turned to Agatha. "I thought you were so cool, the way you took on that security guard by yourself."

Agatha felt of ping of pride before she reminded herself that Nathan said *thought*—past tense. As in, not thinking it anymore.

"Obviously it was Orville who gave up the names," Stu said. "He's too stupid to lie."

Agatha wasn't going to let the conversation go there, even if Orville didn't seem to mind. "Look, you guys. Orville's system wasn't defective. Someone else set the fire in the field house. It was a separate fire," she said.

Jack spoke for the first time. "Come on. That doesn't make much sense."

"It really doesn't," Lissa agreed.

Agatha glanced over at Orville and WHAM! It was like some of his smarts got zapped into her head, because suddenly she got it. "I'll tell you how it makes sense. Somebody else set that fire. Somebody who wanted the Monsters to get blamed for it!"

They all rolled their eyes. "But how could anyone be sure that we'd get blamed?" Nathan asked. "Nobody knew about our prank plans. They were top secret."

"Yeah, but word always leaks out," Jack put in. "Remember last year? The whole school knew that we hid the Shark players' uniforms. Someone at Placid could have heard us talking about it or something."

"I don't buy it," Stu said, staring at Agatha. "Admit it. You and the mutant just screwed up."

Agatha stepped close enough to Stu to smell the breakfast burrito on his breath. "Call him a mutant or any variation thereof again, and your nose will be bleeding until we graduate," she informed him calmly, using all her will to keep the rumbling volcano inside her from erupting.

Then she backed up so she could address the larger group. "I will prove to you that Orville and I are not responsible for this fire. I just need a little time. So this is what's going to happen." She began ticking off the points of her plan on her fingers. "You guys will help Orville and me sneak out of detention today. He and I are going to investigate the field house. We are going to find out who set it on fire. We are going to bring back solid evidence. We are going to clear all our names and make sure that John Q. still gets to use the field."

She met the gaze of each person in the group. "Does anyone have a problem with that?" she asked.

Unfortunately, no one seemed impressed by her tough-guy act. "Yeah, I have a problem," Lissa said. "Now that I have detention, I'm ineligible for student government office. You guys got me fired from being president. So frankly, I really don't feel like helping you do anything." She spun around and stalked down the hall. Agatha gulped down the humiliation that stabbed through her. She looked at the others.

"No way," Nathan said. "You snitched on us. And you screwed up the only thing I care about in this whole school—*football*. I'm not helping."

Stu just snorted and walked away.

Trembling, Agatha turned to Jack.

He stared back seriously. "Why did you tell on us?"

"Orville can't lie," Agatha admitted. "He just . . . can't."

Jack nodded. "Okay. I'll help you."

"Thank you," Agatha breathed. "We'll find out who really did it, I promise."

"You'd better," Jack said. "Or Nathan and I can kiss football goodbye. Coach Pettit told us we're off the team."

"How is there a team if there's no field?" Agatha asked.

"There's still a team. And if I show up at high school without a recommendation from the coach, I don't play. And he's not going to recommend someone he's booted." Jack walked away, leaving Agatha staring after him.

"Why did you tell them we'd find out who set the fire?" Orville asked. "It's highly improbable that we'll be able to do that."

"I know," Agatha whispered. "What have I gotten us into?"

No homework, Orville reminded himself as he sat in detention after school that day. *And no head calculations for fun.* Agatha didn't want him to get distracted and miss "go time."

A spitball hit him on the side of the head. He peeled it off his cheek and stared at it. How much did the moisture affect the velocity? *Stop it!* a voice in his head (a voice that sounded like Agatha's) scolded. *No calculations!*

"No spitballs!" Ms. Winogrand, the detention monitor,

exclaimed. "They are rude! They are disrespectful! They are unsanitary! And. I. Will. Not. Have. Them."

A spitball landed in Ms. Winogrand's permanganate-colored hair. Agatha always called Ms. Winogrand's hair the color someone's poop would be if they ate Barney the dinosaur for dinner. But permanganate was more accurate. Permanganate ions absorb green light, and what is left of the spectrum appears intensely purple.

"Who did that?" Ms. Winogrand screeched. She clawed at the moist ball of paper and saliva with both hands. "Who. Did. That?"

If she had left the spitball in place, I could have done calculations to determine its flight path, Orville thought. *Maybe . . .*

"Stu did it," Jack called.

"No way!" Stu yelled.

Orville flipped open his binder. His pen began to move across the page.

"One at a time," Ms. Winogrand ordered from somewhere far away.

Then the room went silent. Orville's vision filled with the white paper, straight blue lines, and numbers and symbols marching across them. *Yeah, yeah*, Orville thought. *Almost got it.*

BAM! The denim cover of Orville's binder slammed shut, breaking his pencil. "Get up, Orville!" Agatha whispered. "For the love of all that's right and good!"

Orville stood up. He realized that things in the room

were different. Stu's desk was on the ground. So was Stu. And Jack was on top of him. And the other kids were chanting, "Fight! Fight! Fight!" And Ms. Winogrand was alternately pulling at Jack and pulling at Stu, trying to wrench them apart.

Orville got it. It was "go time." Agatha had convinced Jack to help them sneak out, so Jack had picked a fight with Stu. Causing a distraction was a classic battle maneuver. The detention monitor was paying no attention to them at all.

Orville stuffed his binder into his backpack and followed Agatha out of the classroom as fast as his feet could carry him. They ran straight out to the bike racks.

"No calculations. Didn't I beg you no calculations?" Agatha asked as she unlocked her bike.

"I didn't mean to," Orville told her as he dialed in his bike lock combination—8-19-18-71—aviator Orville Wright's birthday.

"I know, I know." Agatha climbed on her bike. "It's hard being a genius."

Orville mounted his own bike without telling her that her left eyelid was more vanadium (III) gray than the other one. He'd learned from her that sometimes girls wore makeup—which made their faces unnatural colors in unusual places. Agatha had never worn makeup before. She must be trying something new. Unlike him, she wasn't afraid to do that.

"What am I supposed to do when we get to the Placid school?" he asked as they pedaled away.

"We suss things out," Agatha called. "We dig the dirt, we get the skinny, um, we snoop around, um . . . Okay, you got me, I don't know what we do, Orville."

She started pedaling faster. "I just shot off my mouth. I was so mad at them for not believing we didn't start that fire. It was wrong for them to blame us without any proof—so I said we would find out who did it. I must have been out of my mind!"

Orville's heart began to beat faster than it usually did at this speed on this stretch of road. He wanted to ask Agatha again what he was supposed to do when they got to the Placid school. But she'd already said she didn't know.

He focused on pedaling, and his heartbeat slowed down when they passed the sign that read Placid: A Nice Little Town Owned by Alfred L. Placid.

The streets of Placid were smooth and black, with white lines that always looked freshly painted. No potholes. No cracks in the sidewalks, either. Orville approved. So did his mother. She was always saying how much she wanted to sell real estate in Placid instead of Bottomless Lake. She wanted to live in Placid, too. But Orville didn't. He could never give up Agatha. Not even for perfect right angles, aerodynamic streets and sidewalks, and logically named streets. Never.

Agatha explained things to him. Plus she understood him—better than anyone else Orville knew. Even his mother didn't take the time to look at things Orville found interesting. But Agatha didn't mind. Lots of times, she found them interesting too.

"You're better than Placid," Orville told his best friend as they pulled up to the Placid Middle School bike racks.

"Thanks." Agatha laughed. "You too." She caught sight of her face in her bike's side view mirror. "Hey, why didn't you tell me my eye shadow was lopsided?"

Orville shrugged.

Agatha rubbed some of the gray off her left eyelid, then looked down at her feet. "I wish I'd known we were coming here. I would have worn my red shoes."

"The shoes you're wearing aren't as safe as the red ones," Orville agreed. "The red shoes have a finely structured tread that runs perpendicular to the longitudinal axis of the sole. All my shoes do. It gives a better grip. But the school grounds here are very well maintained—better than our school's. You should be okay."

"Cuter, Orville. My red shoes are cuter," Agatha told him.

Orville shrugged. There were times when he gave Agatha key pieces of data and she didn't even flip open a notebook.

"So what I'm thinking is, uh, we interview suspects," Agatha announced.

"Who are they?" Orville asked.

"We don't have any yet," Agatha admitted. "But they're at this school somewhere. I'm sure one of these Shark kids set the fire to make our school look bad."

"How do you know?" Orville asked.

"It just seems like something the Sharks would do. I'm using female intuition. Or spider sense. Or my gut. Or I have no idea what I'm doing." Agatha rubbed her face with both hands. "Let's just look around. I'm hoping we'll find some people doing after-school stuff."

"Odds are good there will be people around at this time of day," Orville reassured her.

They walked up the flagstone pathway to the wide double doors. The columns on either side were Doric, according to his mother. She approved of the design for this school building. She thought that "classic surroundings set the atmosphere for learning."

His father had never said anything about the Placid school. Or the town. His father didn't talk much, except to Esther and Jeremy, the pigs he trained for the underwater show at The Grotto. The ratio of words Orville and his father spoke combined—including the words spoken to the pigs—to the words his mother spoke was, on average, 3.3 to 7.4.

Agatha used both hands to shove open the door. She didn't use the bar—she pressed on the glass, leaving double handprints behind her.

"Which way first?" she asked when they stood in the center of the marble floor of the lobby.

Orville shrugged.

"Don't give me that." Agatha shrugged back at him. "There's no right answer. Just pick."

One thing about Agatha, she didn't let him just follow along. A lot of people assumed that was all Orville *could* do. "Left," Orville said.

Agatha spun on her heel and headed left. "We're looking for people of any kind," she said. "Well, not teachers. Or the principal. Normal people."

"I hear chess up there," Orville told her. He took the lead, steering toward the sound.

"You can *hear* chess?" Agatha asked.

Orville opened a classroom door. *Thwap! Thwap! Thwap-thwap-thwap!* Players hit chess clocks all over the room.

"This is a scary, scary sight." Agatha's eyes darted from clock to clock as hands slapped down on them over and over.

"It's just speed chess. There is an extremely small danger quotient." Orville rubbed the tiny scar on his chin. "With these players," he added.

"That was five years ago," Agatha protested. "And you know I wasn't aiming at you. The horse ricocheted."

"Knight," Orville corrected.

"I'm going in." Agatha straightened her shoulders and

strode over to the closest table. "Were you two at the football game on Saturday?" she demanded. "I need to know if you saw anyone hanging around the field house."

Neither of the chess players looked up. Orville caught sight of the series of chess moves written on the chalkboard—e4, d5, exd5, Qxd5, Nc3. The notations brought up a chessboard in his mind. He made the five moves in his imagination, then tried to decide what he'd do next. . . .

A snapping sound caught his attention. Orville blinked and realized Agatha was standing in front of him, snapping her fingers. His mother didn't like it when Agatha did that, but Orville did because it worked. He and Agatha had come up with the system back in third grade. It was how she could get his attention when he was busy concentrating on something else. Finger snapping got his attention immediately because it was something he could never make his own fingers do. They rubbed together, and it even hurt a little. But they never made a sound.

"Good, you're back among the living." She led the way out into the hall. "Want a recap?" Agatha didn't wait for him to answer. "While you were off in The Brain, I was asking people if they had seen anything strange before the fire started. And guess what? Every single person in that room told me they knew exactly how the fire started."

"How?" Orville asked. He noticed that one of the sparkly pink stones had fallen out of Agatha's earrings.

"The stupid prank the Monsters pulled started it!" Agatha answered. "EVERYONE thinks that we're responsible for this fire! Why did I drag us over here? I'm no detective."

"Can I help you two with something?" a man wearing a bow tie asked as he walked toward them.

"We were just leaving," Agatha told him. She started back down the hall, then turned around suddenly. Orville stopped short. He nearly bumped into her— breaking the no-touching zone! It was a close call.

"Actually," Agatha addressed the man again, "I'm looking for my friend Samantha Boutry. She works at your school TV station. Can you tell me where it is?"

"Of course," the man answered. "Take the stairs across from the main entrance and turn right. It's the second door on the left. I believe a few students are still working up there."

Agatha thanked the man, and the two of them took off.

"Teachers seem more . . . trusting here," Agatha commented as they retraced their steps to the lobby.

"Security cameras." Orville pointed out the nearest one.

"Oh." Agatha smiled. "As always, it's good to have you with me, Orville."

He and Agatha started up the staircase. Their footsteps

echoed on the heavy marble. Agatha wasn't holding the handrail. Orville thought she should be, since she wasn't wearing the shoes with the best tread.

"Orville, do you think everyone can tell I'm a Bottomless Lake girl just by looking at me?" Agatha asked when they reached the top of the stairs.

"Everyone?" Orville asked. There were definitely entire countries he could rule out.

As if she could read his mind, Agatha shook her head. "Everyone in Placid. Do you think everyone in Placid can tell? Forget about it being a small town where everyone knows everyone. Is there something about me that screams out not-Placid?"

Thousands of images rushed through Orville's mind. All kinds of observations about girls he'd made from both towns. To sort them, to categorize them . . . He felt like his brain was going to melt down.

"Never mind. Stupid question," Agatha said, pulling Orville back out of his thoughts. "And anyway, I didn't even tell you the flash of brilliance I got downstairs. We don't need to ask people around here what they saw. Everyone in Placid wants this to be the Monsters' fault anyway. I'm thinking we should get a copy of the tape of the football game that Samantha made for Shark TV! After all, pictures don't lie! The tape can help us figure out what *really* happened."

Agatha stopped in front of the second door on the

left. "Um, Orville," she whispered, "speaking of lying, I'm going to have to lie a little, fib, really, when we go in here. Don't disagree with me, okay? Or just try not to."

Orville didn't answer. He wasn't sure how he could *try* not to disagree with Agatha. If someone asked him a question, he would have to answer it, wouldn't he?

She opened the door. "This is the TV station, right?"

"Yep. And those things right over there are TV sets," answered a boy with his bangs plastered to his forehead by some kind of sticky stuff. *The guy with the camera,* Orville thought, remembering him from the game.

"Chet likes to think he's funny," a tall red-haired girl holding a bottle of Evian water said. Orville recognized her too. She was the reporter—Samantha.

"John Q. fans—what a surprise! Come on in," Samantha said.

Agatha and Orville stepped all the way inside and let the door glide shut behind them. It didn't slam the way the doors at John Q. did. There was only the gentle click of the latch.

"You did a great job reporting on the game Saturday," Agatha told Samantha.

Orville started to think about Agatha's previous question. Was there an obvious distinction between girls who went to Placid and girls who went to Bottomless Lake?

The tread on Samantha's shoes would give her a less secure grip than Agatha's. Chet's sneakers had excellent tread—and a piece of banana gum stuck on one heel. *You're comparing girls*, Orville reminded himself.

Samantha stood with her left hand in the pocket of her long, fuzzy red sweater. In the other hand, she held a bottle of Evian. Placid girls drank Evian. Agatha stood with both hands jammed in the pockets of her jeans. As far as Orville knew, she'd never paid for water in her life. She thought it was stupid.

Samantha's eyelids were tan—a darker shade than her skin. Agatha's eyelids were gray. Samantha had a Band-Aid on the back of her hand. Agatha had a scrape on her arm—no Band-Aid. Chet had a burn mark on his thumb. *Forget about Chet*, Orville reminded himself.

Samantha had a tiny hole in one of her red socks. Agatha had a rip in the knee of her jeans. Samantha—

Snap! "We should get going, Orville."

He blinked. Wasn't Agatha going to try and get the tape of the— Then he saw the tape in Agatha's hand. Samantha was now sitting on the counter by one of the TV monitors, still with her left hand in her pocket but without the bottle of water. When he'd started focusing on details, he hadn't noticed anyone moving around or talking. Sometimes he just thought too hard. That's what everybody said.

He turned around and reached for the doorknob, but the door swung open before he could touch it. A girl walked into the room. She wore her brown hair in a bunch of knots all over her head. Her tennis shoe had a small grass stain on the side. Orville thought he'd seen her at the snack stand during the football game too. Yeah. She'd had a droplet of nail polish on her knee. He remembered her because it was weird.

"They were just leaving," Samantha quickly told the girl.

"Well, thanks," Agatha said.

"Whatever," Samantha told Agatha. Rolling her eyes, she herded them out the door—and shut it in Orville's face.

"Jeez, Samantha practically pushed us out of there," Agatha complained. "She didn't bother to introduce us to her friend or anything. And she was all nice before."

"You got what you wanted, right?" Orville asked, checking to make sure Agatha still had the videotape in her hand.

Agatha sighed. "Yeah. But it's still not fun to get what Uncle Jim calls 'the bum's rush.'" Then she smiled. "How brilliant am I to think of getting this tape, though? Our work here is almost done. I just want to stop by the scene of the crime. All detectives do that, I'm pretty sure."

Two minutes and fifty-three seconds later, by Orville's internal clock, they were at the remains of the field house. Only one wall still stood—the rest of the walls were crumbled black bumps on the ground. The horrible scent from Saturday lingered there. It was almost overpowering.

"Stu was right about the cow poop smell, but now it's two-day-old, *burnt* cow poop," Agatha said. She stepped between the field house's miniature Doric columns. They were blackened but still standing.

Orville picked his way around the columns and scanned the ground. Many types of balls had survived the fire. Well, not survived, exactly, but they were still recognizable. He nudged a deflated soccer ball with his toe. It was more black than black and white now, but you could still tell what it had been.

"It's like it's been skinned." Agatha's nose wrinkled. "I wish we had a rake to comb through the ash. It would be faster."

"Are we looking for something that small?" Orville asked.

"I don't know," Agatha admitted. "I'm figuring we're looking for something out of place. Or something clue-ish. Ooh! Like that!" She swooped down and grabbed a twisted piece of turquoise-colored plastic approximately seven-and-a-half-centimeters long and three millimeters thick.

Agatha did her happy dance. "Soccer ball skin. Toasted lacrosse stick. Piece of turquoise plastic. One of these things is not like the others! Let's look for more."

"I haven't found anything else," Agatha announced 6.3 minutes later. And 2.4 minutes after that. And eighteen seconds after that. And seven seconds after that. And fourteen seconds after that. And twenty-two seconds after that. She had covered the field house five times before Orville made it through once.

"What are we doing? We're not *CSI: Bottomless Lake*. There's no way we're going to find anything else. Our job here is done," Agatha pronounced. "Let's go."

Orville started across the ashy floor toward the scorched field. His right foot slid on something slick. Nothing the tread of his shoe couldn't handle. He reached down to see what it was. More plastic—a much larger piece, thirteen-and-a-half centimeters by nine centimeters. Gray in color. Too thin to accurately measure. Flexible. With about a nine-centimeter slice across it.

"Look at this," Orville called. Agatha backtracked over to him. "This is thin plastic, like a bag," he said.

"But what kind of bag?" Agatha asked.

Orville stared at the plastic in his hand. He could barely make out some letters printed on it: G-O-A . . .

"Oh my gosh!" Agatha shouted—so loud it hurt Orville's ear. "Go and Grow! My Uncle Jack uses it in his garden. This was a giant bag of fertilizer!"

"Fertilizers have a high concentration of ammonium nitrate," Orville said. "That makes them extremely flammable."

"So the fertilizer is what burned down the field house," Agatha said, her eyes wide with excitement.

"This slit in the plastic is very uneven," Orville said. "This bag was not opened correctly."

Agatha studied the slice in the bag. "You're right. It kind of looks like somebody stuck a spoon in it and just pulled it apart from there."

"I don't think a spoon would be the proper—" Orville began.

"Ohmigod," Agatha gasped, interrupting him. "Gardening chemicals that have been ripped open? This is our first step toward proving arson. Now we just have to figure out who did it!"

Orville stood up straight the way Miss Eloise had taught him to when he had something important to say. Social skills class was big on the proper use of body language. And what he had to say was very important—*he knew without a doubt who had set the fire.*

"Badge of Bravery!" Agatha burst out.

"What?" Orville asked.

"Badge of Bravery," Agatha repeated, "that true crime book I snuck out of Nana's bookshelf last summer. I stopped reading it around the middle because I had those nightmares. Anyway, it told all about how the cops tracked down their perp. Now that we have a lead, we have to do what they did! Okay, we need to think about motive and opportunity. Our perpetrator will need a motive for starting the fire, and they need to have had the opportunity to get into the field house and do it."

"What kinds of motive—" Orville began.

"Just let me get this all out before I forget," Agatha

interrupted, beginning to pace. "The rules are: we have to make a list of suspects. I bet the tape will help with that. Then we'll work on our suspects' motives and opportunity, but no matter what we do, we can't accuse anyone until we find the evidence to back it up."

Evidence? Motive? Orville sighed. He didn't have any of that. And according to Agatha, that meant he couldn't accuse anyone. So he couldn't tell Agatha who had done it.

He was pretty sure his perpetrator had the opportunity to set the field house on fire. Motive . . . he wasn't so sure about. Motive was all about emotional reasons for doing things. And emotions were the most confusing things Orville had ever encountered.

He wished he could talk all this through with Agatha. But she said he couldn't make an accusation without evidence.

The big problem was he knew with one hundred percent certainty who the arsonist was.

But he had no idea *how* he knew.

Chapter 4

"RED ALERT! My grandmother is home! It's during shop hours and my nana is *home*. This is bad, Orville. Very, very bad." Agatha gulped. "No matter what happens, just let me handle this."

She bounded across the small front lawn and burst through the front door of her grandmother's house. "Hi, Nana!" She gave her short, squat grandmother a big hug and a smacking kiss on the cheek.

"No," Nana Wong said.

That was it. Just "no."

"Um, Orville's with me," Agatha pointed out, hoping Nana wouldn't slice and dice her—which she was clearly dying to do—in front of her friend. "We're going to do some homework. Did you need something? Let me help you find it. You must have to get back to the shop."

Nana Wong was dressed in her work clothes—a kimono. It wasn't a Chinese outfit, but her grandmother claimed it gave off an exotic Asian feel. A lot of the tourists looking for Trixie liked anything they thought was exotic—somehow Asian mystery and sea monster lore worked well together. That's why Nana

Wong always wore her hair in a geisha-type knot on the top of her head.

Then, for the tourists who wanted the whole Arizona-slash-Western thing, Agatha's nana wore red cowboy boots and lots of Native American jewelry. She switched between the two each day.

"What a considerate granddaughter," Nana Wong answered. "You're right, Agatha. I should be at the shop. I should be earning money. You know how many grandchildren I have. You know how many years of college I might have to pay for. But instead, I'm here. And do you know *why* I'm here?"

Agatha knew better than to answer that question.

"I am here because your principal called me. He told me that you burned down a building!" Nana Wong whipped her head toward Orville, nailing him with her mean-hyena-spots-poor-wounded-gazelle glare. "And don't think I haven't heard about *your* part in this too."

"You closed down the shop because the principal called you about the fire?" Orville asked.

"I didn't close down. I left Cousin Darrell in charge," Nana Wong answered. She whipped her head back toward Agatha. "And you know your cousin Darrell. He'll have his friends in there by now, and my Trixie figurines will be out of their case and under attack by some Orc dolls."

"Action figures. They're called *action figures*," Agatha blurted. (Cousin Darrell was such a geek.) "And the fire that burned down the field house was a completely separate one from the little, totally controlled fire that was part of our prank. We didn't burn down anything!"

"It's impossible," Orville agreed.

Agatha's grandmother sat down in her favorite chair—a Barcalounger. She didn't lean back in the red leather cushions, and she didn't pull the lever that would let her put her feet up. But she looked ready to hear their side—in a Judge Judy kind of way.

Agatha pulled in a deep breath—and Orville started to talk. "You left Darrell in charge even though you know he'll be playing in your shop? And that's because the principal called about the fire and you wanted to talk to Agatha right away?" he asked.

Why is he picking today to start being a conversationalist? Agatha moaned to herself. She didn't give her grandmother a chance to answer Orville. She began talking before he had completely stopped, giving Nana the rundown on the safety of the prank.

"Orville calculated everything. . . . The fire started 5.3 seconds after ours. . . . There wasn't enough fuel for a spark to reach the field house. . . ." It all poured out of Agatha so fast, she hardly thought about what she was saying.

"So it really wasn't our fault at all," Agatha concluded. She stared at her grandmother, waiting for judgment, her bones vibrating with anxiety.

"I think Orville needs to go home," Nana Wong said. "And *you* need to go to your room and wait while I call your parents. This isn't a decision a grandmother can make."

No. No, no, *no!* Her parents would put her under house arrest until they got back from Russia—and Agatha had to catch the person who truly started the fire! She threw herself to her knees at the foot of the Barcalounger. "Wait! A couple of days, that's all I'm asking. A couple of days so Orville and I can prove who really burned down the field house."

Nana Wong raised an eyebrow. "So you're detectives now? Who do you think you are? Sergeant Schiff from *Badge of Bravery?*"

"Yes!" Agatha said. She dug through her backpack and pulled out the videotape. "I was late getting home because Orville and I have already started our investigation." Her words crashed into each other like bumper cars. "We got this tape of the football game. It will have the fire on it. We're going to watch it and come up with a list of suspects. Oh, and look. We've got evidence!"

Triumphantly she pulled the twisted piece of charred turquoise-colored plastic out of her backpack. It didn't look that impressive, especially because the piece of plastic had become tangled in the strands of hair caught in her hairbrush.

Nana Wong gave a grunt of disapproval. *I should probably clean my brush a little more often*, Agatha thought.

"That's not all. Orville, show Nana the really important piece of important forensic material, incriminating, important proof that we have," Agatha begged.

Orville slid the flexible piece of gray plastic out of his backpack. A mix of ash and some kind of day-old-burnt-cow-poop-smelling liquid began to drip on Nana Wong's white shag rug.

"Out in the front yard, Orville!" Agatha ordered. "Right now, if you value your life."

Orville hurried out. Agatha braced her hands on each of the armrests of the Barcalounger so her grandmother couldn't stand up. "I know you're about to go extremely mental, Nana. But I need you to listen. This isn't me trying to get out of detention or whatever punishment my parents come up with. This is about the next five years of my life. No, it's about the rest of my *entire* life. Because if you don't let me clear our names, I will be so damaged by the end of high school, I'll be worse than Cousin Eleanor."

A worried expression crossed Nana's face. Cousin Eleanor was twenty-seven. She still lived at home and worked part-time. Her last position had been as a cashier at the Gas 'N' Sip. She'd only lasted there for half a day.

Nana leaned back in her chair. "I'm listening."

"Orville and I, we were okay before we were invited to help with the prank. We flew under the radar. Then I was sure that we—or at least I, because Orville couldn't care less—had found one of the tickets to the silver bird of popularity. I was in. I was gonna be the coolest of the cool."

Her grandmother made a *pish* sound.

"Never mind. Not important." Agatha tightened her grip on the chair. "What's important is that now, in one day, we're not even fringe dwellers. We're the unclean. We're pariahs. Untouchables. People swerve to avoid us in the halls. Even the nice ones. You don't want to know what the other ones do."

Nana Wong leaned forward. Agatha kept talking. "And you know what? They're right. Because they believe we did something that got the school president kicked out of office. They believe that because of our actions, nobody is going to get to play football, or soccer, anything involving a field, ever again. And no one is ever, ever going to forget."

Tears stung her eyes. She willed them to stop. She had held out in school. You didn't cry in school. You didn't. But here, where she felt safe . . .

Agatha blinked hard, trying to somehow suction the

tears back, but they wouldn't stop. She furiously swiped them away with her sleeve. "We didn't do it, Nana."

There was a long silence. Then: "You pay for the Trixies your cousin Darrell breaks. You get that stain off the carpet—start with salt." Nana Wong stood up and easily pushed past Agatha, proving she'd never been a prisoner. "And you have until your parents get home to play Nancy Drew, Scooby-Doo, whatever."

Agatha leapt to her feet and hugged her grandmother. This time she got a hug back, one of Nana Wong's rib-bruising specials.

"You can go back in now, Orville," Nana Wong called as she marched out of the house. "Just leave that nasty plastic outside."

As soon as they got the stain out of the carpet— which wasn't as hard as Agatha thought it would be, because Orville used some kind of chemistry magic— they popped the video into Nana's old VCR.

They only watched for three seconds before Agatha pushed pause. "One sec." She dug into her backpack for her Spider-Man notebook and flipped to a clean page. "I'm going to make a list of suspects. If we're going to solve this case, we've got to start acting like professionals. Like the evidence should go in plastic bags. They had bags in *Badge of Bravery*." She hit play.

Agatha leaned forward, eyes locked on the TV. She

was afraid to blink. She didn't want to miss *anything.* Her fingers started to ache from gripping her pen so hard. She wanted to write something down in the Spider-Man notebook now!

"Wow! Orville!" she suddenly exclaimed.

"What? Do you see something?"

"I see *us.*" She pointed to the screen, where Samantha was interviewing Lissa about the Sharks' new uniforms. Orville and Agatha were sitting next to her—Kit and Edmundo on Agatha's other side—and they so looked like they belonged. Right here on TV was proof that for one day, or part of one day, she and Orville had made it into the cool crowd.

The Monster cheerleaders finished their "Red Hot" cheer. The camera swung around to catch the Shark squad starting the cheer Agatha hated about pumping gas. She continued to study the screen. The camera lingered on one face, and a lightbulb went off in Agatha's brain.

"Orville, we have found a suspect!" she said, leaping from the couch. "And I know her motive and everything!"

"You do?" Orville had been running his hands through his sandy brown hair and now it was standing on end. It had gotten way too long. Agatha made a mental note to go with him to get it cut.

Orville's mother always made him get the same cut he'd had when he was five. And his father probably wouldn't have noticed if his hair reached his butt. Orville's dad was great. But he didn't notice things like hair.

"Yep, I do, mister," Agatha answered. "Our first suspect is—*ding, ding, ding*—Tina Gore! Matthew Lopez broke her heart. *Monster football player* Matthew Lopez. Monster football player Matthew Lopez who refused to take Tina to the Enchanted Lake Dance after he asked her and she bought a new dress—all because the coach told him he needed to focus on football. Matthew Lopez chose football over love. And Tina got honey-sweet revenge: Matthew won't be playing this year—because the field is toast."

"Motive—revenge," Orville said slowly.

"Right," Agatha answered. "Now, when we get close to the part where the fire starts, we have to watch Tina. She has motive, but we don't know about opportunity. If she's in plain sight when the field house goes up in smoke, she can't go on our list."

Agatha turned her full attention back to the TV. The Shark players were taking the field one by one. Then the game began.

"Oh, no, Jack, don't do it," Agatha couldn't help crying out in the first quarter. Of course it didn't have any effect. A second later, Jack handed the ball off to a Shark. "What happened to him on Saturday?" she asked.

"Statistically, his play during the first half of the

game was within his usual range," Orville told her. "Length of throws. Passes completed."

"But to the wrong team." Agatha shook her head. "It's like he wanted to help the Sharks." She grabbed one of the red leather throw pillows and pressed it against her stomach. "Uh-oh."

"What?"

"Uh-oh." She clutched the pillow tighter against her belly.

"Are you going to vomit?" Orville looked anxious.

"No, I'm not going to vomit," Agatha snapped. "But thank you for your concern," she added more gently. Then she bit her lip. "It's just that, what if Jack *was* helping the Sharks during the game? I can't believe it, but what if he was? Maybe he helped them at halftime too! Maybe he has to be on our suspect list!"

"We're up to the halftime show." Orville nodded toward the TV. "We have to watch for opportunity."

"Right," Agatha answered. She forced herself to sit up straight.

The Shark cheerleading squad did their number. Tina wasn't in it. And she never came back onto the field before the bleachers were evacuated.

"Tina the Heartbroken is absolutely a suspect." Agatha wrote Tina's name down in her notebook. "And so is Jack. Both football teams were off the field during halftime."

Agatha added Jack's name to her list and sighed. "I don't want to do this," she said, thinking out loud. "But if I have to take him downtown, I will."

"Downtown where?" Orville asked.

"I just mean the principal's office," Agatha explained.

"That's not downtown. It's two degrees west and seven degrees south of downtown," he corrected.

"Good to know." Agatha threw down the red pillow. "Well, let's get to work, Orville. We've got an arsonist to find!"

Agatha noticed Ms. Winogrand staring at Orville from behind her desk the next day. He was using detention to make one of his crazy complicated paper airplanes. Agatha knew it was one of the Wright Brothers' planes, but she wasn't sure which one. Maybe the Jonahed Flyer?

Agatha had watched pretty much every aviation documentary and movie known to man with Orville. It helped her to understand him at times like this.

Another quick check showed that Ms. Winogrand was still studying Orville. No surprise. After all, his planes *were* cool. Agatha took the opportunity to toss the help-us-sneak-out-again note she'd written to Jack. He was sitting three desks away. Orville was the only person who was actually sitting next to her.

Everyone else seemed to think that unpopularity was contagious.

The answer from Jack came back almost immediately. *Got extra day of Ms. Wino for fight yesterday. Parents will exterminate if I get more. Sorry.*

Agatha looked over at Jack to give him a nod of understanding. But he was bent low over his homework.

Got it, Agatha thought. *He's willing to be nice, if it doesn't cost him anything. If no one is looking.* Clearly she and Orville would be—

"You!" Ms. Winogrand called, jerking Agatha out of her thoughts. The detention monitor strode up to Orville. Agatha scooted her desk closer. She was prepared to explain that his paper airplane was for a science project, and she would have to do it before her friend "Honest Abe" could admit he was making it for fun. Fun was not allowed in detention.

"Were you here yesterday?" Ms. Winogrand demanded. "I don't have any new students in detention today. That means you should have been here yesterday. But I don't remember you."

Uh-oh. Trouble ahead!

"He's very quiet—" Agatha began.

"I want *you* quiet," Ms. Winogrand interrupted. Her purple hair almost glowed under the fluorescent lights.

"Well?" she asked Orville.

Incoming disaster bomb, Agatha thought.

"I was here for five minutes, and then I snuck out," Orville answered calmly.

Oh, Orville, Agatha silently wailed. *Why do you always do this?*

"To. The. Principal's. Office. *March!*" Ms. Winogrand ordered.

Orville got the goin'-to-the-principal *oooh*.

Agatha got a brilliant idea.

She waited about fifteen seconds. As she waited, she tried to twist her face into the expression her five-year-old cousin Emily got when she had been found using the toilet for Barbie's hot tub. She stood up and shuffled over to Ms. Winogrand's desk. "Um, I have to tell you something."

Ms. Winogrand shoved the horror novel she'd been hiding in her lap into the top drawer of her desk. She slammed the drawer so fast that she caught her finger.

"No one gets up from their desk without permission," she barked. She jerked her finger free and stuck it in her mouth.

"I just wanted to say that, um . . ." Agatha looked down at her feet the way Emily had in the toilet-hot-tub situation. "I snuck out yesterday too." She bit the inside of her cheek hard, trying to force a few tears. They wouldn't come.

"To. The. Principal's. Office!" Ms. Winogrand bellowed.

Agatha ran from the room. She raced toward

Principal Rothman's office. And stopped Orville three steps before he reached the door. "Come on," she whispered. "We're going to Placid."

Orville was still arguing as they pedaled into the town. "It *is* logical. When the principal and Ms. Winogrand are in the same room, there is a reasonable chance they will discover that we didn't follow Ms. Winogrand's instructions."

"Ms. Winogrand is going to be too busy thinking about her horror novel to be worried about us," Agatha reassured him.

She pedaled faster. She wanted to get in and out of Placid as quickly as possible. All that sameness gave her the wiggins. Hadn't Alfred L. ever heard of a curve? Straight line. Straight line. Big square houses. Bigger square lawns. Hedges trimmed so not a leaf was out of place. Agatha was surprised that trees were allowed to grow here, since trees weren't square.

When they reached the Placid Middle School bike rack, Agatha slid her bike into one of the slots without bothering to lock it. No one around here would want her old Schwinn with its yellow banana seat, thinning handlebar streamers, and playing cards clipped to the spokes of the wheels. It was so not "Placid." It wasn't even very "Bottomless Lake." But she loved it. It had Agatha style. Plus she hadn't grown enough to convince her parents to buy her a new one.

"Tina Gore, suspect number one, we're comin' at ya," Agatha said. Orville looked at her cute red shoes with approval as they started toward the gym.

"Back to return that tape?"

Agatha turned toward the voice and saw Chet the cameraman heading toward them, equipment on his shoulder. He was wearing a wool hat today. Agatha thought it was a good choice. The plastered-down style he was working yesterday? Not working.

"Samantha said we could keep it," Agatha answered.

"I just figured since neither of our schools is going to be playing football this year, there's not much point in your coach studying the game," Chet said.

"Oh, well, he's really dedicated." She glanced at Orville. There didn't seem to be any truth-spewing about to happen. Just in case, she changed the subject. "What are you filming today?"

"Sam and I are doing a story on how the cheerleaders are feeling about no football this year," Chet answered.

"I guess we're heading in the right direction. We're looking for Tina Gore," Agatha said. She wished she could bring Orville into conversations more. It always felt rude not to. But he had no interest in talking to people he didn't know—unless they happened to hit on a subject that interested him.

"Yep. In fact, here's the gym. And here come the cheerleaders." Chet frowned. "Guess they don't feel like cheering today." Agatha nodded, taking in the slumped shoulders and dejected faces of the squad.

Samantha appeared in the doorway to the gym. "Let's get started, Chet."

"Gotta go. But I see Tina right over there." Chet pointed, then hurried off.

"I hope Tina hasn't heard that she's supposed to hate us for ruining the field." Agatha led the way over to the ex–Monster cheerleader. They'd been in the same Girl Scout troop before The Incident, the one that had led to Agatha turning in her sash and badges.

She stopped in front of Tina, unsure of how to start the . . . interrogation. "Hi," she said, falling back on Orville's standby.

"Hey. Sorry about the crying." Tina wiped at her eyes with a tissue. "Our coach disbanded the squad. No need for cheerleaders if there's no team to cheer for, right?"

"Um, right. Tina, you remember Orville, don't you?" Agatha asked, changing the topic.

"Sure. What are you guys doing here?" Tina dug in her backpack for a fresh Kleenex.

"Are you required to wear your hair in a ponytail or do you wear it that way because you like it?" Orville asked, ignoring Tina's question. "I observed that seventy-eight percent of the Shark cheerleaders have ponytails."

Tina stared at him for a long moment. "Uh, a lot of us wear ponytails because it keeps our hair out of the way. And I do it because I'm growing my hair out and it's at a lot of different lengths right now."

"Your hair will look great longer." Agatha wanted Tina relaxed around her. She figured Tina would let more info spill that way. But before she could ask a single question, Samantha approached, microphone in hand. Chet was close behind, filming away.

"Tina, I see you have buddies from Bottomless Lake visiting. That must make you feel nice and comfy." Samantha smirked into the camera.

A cheerleader with black hair cropped close to her head overheard Samantha's comment and snickered.

Tina's eyes narrowed. "Why is that funny, Rose?"

Rose gave a small shrug. "I just think if I were, say, a mouse, I'd be happier in a group of other mice. I wouldn't be comfortable in a roomful of cats." She turned away and began a series of stretches.

"Don't mind Rose," Samantha said. "It's just that when you grow up in a certain place, it leaves a mark on you. But that's not a bad thing. I mean, that's part of what makes us unique. You and Agatha and Orville will always be from Bottomless Lake. I bet you still hang out with a lot of people from over there, don't you?"

"Do you, Tina?" Agatha jumped in. Samantha had given her the perfect opportunity to ask exactly the question she needed to. "Who do you still see from school? Do you still hang out with Kit and Edmundo? Do you have a new boyfriend from there?"

"Here's my question for you, Tina," Samantha cut in. "Do you think *you* feel as bad about the damage to our school as girls who have lived here all their lives?"

"Of course! I feel horrible!" Tina began to back away from Orville and Agatha. "I love Placid! I love our school! Why can't you all just accept me?" she choked out. Then she turned and raced back into the gym.

Samantha gave the cut sign to Chet. "Sorry." She pushed her hair away from her face and smiled at Agatha. "I guess it might have seemed like I was harshing on your town. I just need a good sound bite. The sobbing might work."

"Why do you smile three times more often when you're on camera than when you're off?" Orville asked.

"Part of the job. See you!" Samantha headed toward another cheerleader.

With a wave to Orville and Agatha, Chet followed.

Agatha shook her head. "Samantha Boutry is the most two-faced person I have ever met."

"As far as I can tell, she only has one face," Orville stated.

"You're certainly chatty today," Agatha commented, turning to Orville. "If I could do the calculations like you, I'd say that you've used one hundred and three percent more words than usual today. What's with all the questions?"

"A hundred and five per—" Orville began.

"It doesn't matter," Agatha interrupted. "Why did you ask Tina about her hair?"

"Why did you ask her about her friends at John Q.?" Orville countered.

"Because whoever burned down the field house knew about our prank," Agatha explained. "They knew exactly where it was going to be and when it was going to be. They knew it was going to involve fire. So I'm thinking maybe a friend of Tina's helped her. Maybe someone on the prank committee gave her all the details."

"Someone in our school needed to help the arsonist?" Orville asked.

"Yeah, we could have a double-agent scenario." Agatha frowned. "Except Tina seemed so upset about the field. She was crying and everything. It's hard to cry on cue. I just tried it in detention, and—"

"I'm eavesdropping," Rose called from the spot on the grass where she was still doing stretches. Agatha turned to her in surprise.

"I don't especially like Tina," Rose said. "But she didn't start the fire."

"How can you know that?" Agatha demanded. Tina was the top suspect.

"Because right before the halftime show, Tina's uniform

zipper broke." Rose bent at the waist, reaching one arm over her head. "Good Samaritan that I am, and because she's my partner in a lift, I tried to help her fix it. I couldn't do it. We were in the locker room through the whole show. We both missed our last chance to perform this year, because the basketball team has different cheer-leaders. So Tina couldn't have set the fire."

"Oh. Thanks." Agatha turned away. An alibi. Tina had an alibi. Agatha let out a long, mournful sigh. "You know what that means."

Orville didn't answer. Maybe she'd freaked him out by mentioning his increased word usage.

"It means . . ." Agatha hesitated, hating to let the words out. "It means that Jack Simmons, Monster foot-ball hero, is now our prime suspect."

Chapter 5

"We have to interrogate Jack today," Agatha said as she and Orville parked their bikes in front of John Q. Middle School. She smelled like Cocoa Puffs again, so her parents were most likely still in Russia. "I need to figure out what his motive is. I mean, if he has one. He might *not* have a motive, because having a motive means . . ."

Agatha kept talking, but the word *motive* sent Orville off into his own thoughts. All last night, he'd thought about his suspect, who he called The One Who Is Innocent Until Proven Guilty. Agatha had said the rules were that he couldn't accuse anyone without motive or evidence, and that meant no accusing, even in his thoughts.

The One Who Is Innocent Until Proven Guilty had opportunity. That much Orville had seen on Samantha's tape. The tape had shown that The One Who Is Innocent Until Proven Guilty was not in the bleachers or on the field when the fire started.

But motive . . . It was like another language.

He'd gone to a chat room for people who read true crime books like the one Agatha was always talking about and asked for their help in understanding what possible motives there were for committing a crime. He'd gotten a bunch of answers—greed, jealousy, hate, love. Then his head had started to hurt and he'd logged off.

Maybe Miss Eloise could help him understand motive when he went to social skills class on Thursday. She was good at explaining things that made no sense. Usually he'd just ask Agatha, but he didn't think he could ask Agatha about this without the possibility of accidentally making the accusation, which wasn't the correct way to—

SNAP! Orville jumped. Obviously he'd tuned out again. Now that Agatha had broken through with her snap maneuver, he realized several things at once. First, they were standing by Agatha's locker. Second, Agatha's cheeks were approximately thirty percent paler than usual. Third, Agatha's breathing was shallow. And fourth, Agatha was trembling.

"Are you cold?" Orville asked. The first thing his brain clicked to was hypothermia, although that made no logical sense. It rarely dropped below seventy degrees in Bottomless Lake at this time of year.

Agatha did show several of the symptoms, but it was unlikely that her core body temperature had dropped to thirty-five degrees Celsius or below.

"No, I'm not cold." Her voice dropped two decibels. "I'm . . . I'm furious. And I'm humiliated. And for the second day in a row, I feel like I'm going to start bawling at school. And I don't cry at school. Ever!"

Agatha stared straight into Orville's eyes. He realized he hadn't said hi that morning. "Hi, Agatha."

Agatha didn't say hi back. What she said was, "You know what the worst thing is? My best friend didn't even realize something was wrong. Even though he was standing right next to me!"

Orville's stomach seized up. He hated this. He hated himself when this happened. Something was wrong with Agatha—and he didn't know what. Other people would know. But he didn't! "What's wrong? I don't—" He pulled in a deep breath, thinking of Miss Eloise's advice about asking people for help when he needed it. "Agatha, I need you to tell me what's wrong."

Agatha swung her locker door all the way open with a bang.

Orville saw a pile of charred newspaper on the locker floor. For the first time, he noticed the scent of smoke, stronger than the curdled milk smell that usually wafted from the cafeteria.

"Look at this. Someone set a fire inside my locker!" Agatha said. "I wonder why they did it? I wonder what their motive was? Hmmm. Maybe to express to me that as a fire starter, I'm not wanted anywhere in this school anymore?" She slammed the metal door closed.

She closed her eyes for a long moment. Her eyelids were just their own color today. But Orville studied them to make sure they were even. If they weren't even, he wanted to tell her, now that he knew she wanted to know. He always did what Agatha wanted. As far as he could tell, best friends did that as much as possible.

But eyelids weren't what was bothering Agatha right now. "You're upset because someone set a fire in your locker." Miss Eloise said sometimes it helped just to repeat back some of what a person said. To show you understood.

Agatha opened her eyes and sighed. "Yes," she answered.

"Is there something I can do?" That was one of the important questions Miss Eloise told him to ask in situations like this. *Now listen to the answer, Orville*, he reminded himself.

"I don't think so," Agatha said. "I'm sorry I yelled. I'm not mad at you. We should go check out your locker. I think some little elves might have visited you too."

"Elves aren't—" Orville began, his stomach still feeling like it was in a six-crossing knot. He'd listened to what she said. But was the part about elves the most important? Or was it the fire? Agatha used so many words, sometimes it was hard to tell.

"You two! Stop. Right. There." Orville knew the voice. Ms. Winogrand. He and Agatha turned to face her. She made a rustling sound as she hurried over to them. Orville identified it as coming from the layers of pink net he could see sticking out from underneath her flowered skirt. The blue flowers pictured were not biologically viable. She wore the skirt with an orange blouse. The combination made Orville's eyes burn a little when he stared at it.

"I talked to Principal Rothman on my way out of the building last night. And I. Know. You. Did. Not. Go. To. His. Office! Why did you disobey me? Why?"

Why . . . The word set Orville's brain buzzing with activity. Motive was why anyone did anything. He wanted to gather as much information about motives as he could. Once he had a large enough sample, he should be able to analyze the data to figure out the motive of The One Who Is Innocent Until Proven Guilty. Maybe Ms. Winograud could help.

"Why did you choose to wear that skirt with that blouse?" Orville asked.

Agatha gave a snort. The kind of snort that was followed by giggles ninety-seven percent of the time. But not this time.

Ms. Winograud's eyes narrowed. She leaned close to Orville—so close she was nearly violating the no-touching zone.

"You two are troublemakers, especially when you are together," Ms. Winograud told them. She buttoned the top button of her blouse. The buttons were shaped like stars. "When you get to detention today, you will sit on opposite sides of the room," she continued. "And there will be no talking to each other. In fact, the two of you should never talk to each other again—*ever!*" She stomped away, her skirt rustling violently.

A moment later, the bell rang. Orville turned toward his next class.

He wanted to say goodbye to Agatha. Sometimes he forgot. But not today. Today he just wasn't allowed. In fact, he wasn't allowed to say anything to Agatha ever again.

But how could that be? What would—? Would she—?

Orville's brain failed him. He couldn't form a complete thought. No Agatha? Since second grade he'd talked to her every day.

How was he supposed to survive without her?

Agatha hurried through the lunch line and over to the table where she and Orville always sat. As soon as she plopped down, he pulled out his foil-wrapped tuna-and-sea-monster-slime sandwich and began to eat.

"Here's the plan. We chow down—then we eliminate another suspect from our list. Then we try to squeeze in locker cleanup, because we have detention after school. I'm assuming your locker was torched, right?"

Orville didn't answer.

Agatha dug into her own lunch. *There he goes again*, she thought. *Lost in his own brain. Maybe he can figure out how to get us out of this whole mess. Or at least get me out of having to interrogate Jack Simmons after lunch.*

"Oh, Oooorrrrville . . ." She sort of sang his name to see if that would get his attention. Then she realized he was looking straight at her—focused—and that he had been the whole time she was talking.

"Orville, did anyone mess up your locker?" she tried again.

No response. Just those eyes looking at her. Pleading with her to understand.

"Orville, what was the name of the Wright Brothers' first plane?" Agatha asked.

Still no response.

Now Agatha was worried. Orville never missed a chance to talk about the Wright Brothers. Back in the second grade, he'd insisted everyone start calling him by his middle name—Orville—instead of his first name, Benjamin. Agatha had tried to convince him it wasn't a smart move. But Orville had always had a mind of his own.

Agatha leaned forward, studying his face. "What is it? Are you sick? Tell me, Orville!"

He handed her a piece of paper. On it, in Orville's neat handwriting, were the words *I can't talk to you.*

"You can't? Why? What's wrong with—?" Agatha stopped mid-sentence. "It's Ms. Winogrand, isn't it?"

Orville wrote *yes* down on the paper.

"Don't worry. Ms. Winogrand never has lunch duty, so it's okay to talk."

He didn't.

"The Wright Brothers' first plane, it was the Dorkmobile, right?" she teased him.

No response.

"Orville, when teachers say things like 'Don't ever talk to each other again,' they don't really mean it. And besides, they can't really ask us to do that. It's unenforceable," Agatha explained.

She was serving it up, but Orville wasn't having any. Well, she would just have to figure out a way to break him down. There was no way she was spending even a few days with Benjamin Orville Wright under the impression he couldn't speak to her. Dealing with her crazy family—and now this school-leper situation—without a hundred percent of her best friend? Uh-uh. She couldn't do it.

"Okay, time to put Jack in the hot seat," Agatha said when Orville finished eating. He always ate slower than she did.

She glanced around the cafeteria, trying to locate her crunch and her number-one suspect. Her heart dropped down to her stomach when she realized Jack was sitting at the popular table. *Of course. Where else would he be?* she thought. *And now I'm going to have to walk right up there and talk to him.*

Her heart and her stomach started to wrestle as she strode over to his table. At least she wasn't alone. Orville was with her, in body if not in voice. The popular table went silent when Agatha stepped up to Jack. "I need to talk to you for a minute. In the hall?"

She turned and headed out of the cafeteria. She wasn't sure if Jack would follow, but he did.

"I heard about what happened to your lockers," he said when the three of them were alone. "It was totally uncalled for."

"Gee, you think?" Agatha shot back. She wanted to be tough while she questioned him. But those few words of sympathy got to her.

"So?" Jack leaned against the nearest row of lockers. "What do you want?"

"We want to talk to you about the day of the fire," Agatha said. "We're still trying to find out what really happened."

"Why not just do the detention? It'll be over fast enough," Jack advised.

"For you," Agatha told him. "Not for me and Orville. Even after detention, no one will forgive us. Besides, no one set your locker on fire, right?"

Jack shook his head.

"And no one blames you for the fact that John Q. has no sports field," Agatha continued. "It's different for us. We have to solve this."

"Do you have a girlfriend?" Orville suddenly asked Jack.

Jack and Agatha both stared at him.

"Uh, no," Jack answered, a flush climbing up his neck.

Agatha decided to ignore Orville's bizarre outburst. "Um, this is kind of an awkward question," Agatha began.

"Do you want a girlfriend?" Orville interrupted.

"I—I guess," Jack said.

Agatha's mind whirled. What was Orville doing?

I have fallen down the rabbit hole, she thought. *And I can't get up.* She held up a finger to Jack. "Give us one second." She backed down the hallway, gesturing for Orville to follow her.

"What are you doing?" she whispered. "Are you trying to hook me and Jack up? Because that's so not going to happen, even if he is the only person in this school who doesn't treat me like I'm a cockroach."

Orville flipped open his notebook. *I'm helping with the case*, he scribbled on the paper.

Agatha sighed. He *still* refused to speak to her. Maybe she could ask Miss Eloise to explain the difference between real rules and not-so-real ones the next time Orville had her class.

"Whatever," Agatha said. She led the way back over to Jack.

"What I wanted to ask was, how were you feeling during the game on Saturday?" Agatha inquired.

"Okay, I guess. I love to play," Jack answered.

Orville butted in. "Can you describe the girlfriend you want?"

Jack's neck flush reached his face. He glanced at Agatha. "Uhhh . . ."

Agatha's face felt as red as Jack's looked. She raced on, ignoring the burning sensation. "I was asking how you were feeling because of, uh, those two, um, mistakes you made. The one where you handed off to a Shark player. And that amazing pass you made . . . to a Shark player."

Orville handed her a note: *Why is your skin redder than it usually is whenever you talk to Jack?*

Agatha crumpled the note and shoved it in the pocket of her cords, praying Jack hadn't been able to read it. Even if he hadn't, she was sure he was thinking she and Orville were a complete freak show by now.

Jack shoved himself away from the lockers. "Why are you asking about those plays? How can that help you figure out who set the fire?"

"The bad plays could lead to an understanding of motive," Orville answered. "If you were helping the Sharks in the game for some reason, maybe you helped them with their prank for the same reason."

Agatha slapped her forehead with her hand. Why couldn't Ms. Wino have told Orville not to talk to *anyone*?

Jack's blue eyes darkened. "Is that what you think?" he asked Agatha. "Here I am defending you when people talk about you behind your back . . . and you think *I* did it?"

He continued before she could answer. "You know, I used to think you were really nice. But now I don't want to talk to you ever again."

Great, Agatha thought. *First Orville, now Jack.*

How much worse could this day possibly get?

Chapter 6

Agatha stared at the clock, waiting for the second hand to make it all the way to the twelve. Less than a minute until detention ended. She couldn't wait to get away from Ms. Winogrand's eyes o' death. Not to mention Jack's.

When the bell rang, Agatha leapt out of her seat and ran for the door. She knew Orville would just take off if she didn't stop him. And during detention she'd found the perfect way to wiggle out of his no-talking rule.

Sure enough, Orville was halfway down the hall by the time she caught up with him. "Hey, wait up!" she yelled. "I have an idea."

Orville stopped walking and turned toward her, but he didn't say a word.

"Ms. Winogrand said we couldn't *talk* to each other, right?"

Orville didn't answer. "Well, how about if you do something else instead?" Agatha rushed on. "Like mumbling or singing or shouting?"

There was a pause as Orville thought about this. Agatha waited.

"YES!" he finally boomed. "I AM ALLOWED TO SHOUT AT YOU!"

A few of the kids from detention snickered as they walked by. Agatha saw Stu roll his eyes. She didn't care. Orville had shouted at her! They were communicating! Now maybe they could get back to clearing their names.

Orville took a deep breath, clearly about to yell something else.

"Wait!" Agatha cried. "Shouting is a little too . . . well, loud. How about whispering? Will that work?"

Orville thought about it again and nodded. "She didn't say no whispering," he whispered.

"Good. Problem solved."

Agatha smiled at her best friend. "I missed you, you know. Don't ever quit talking to me again."

"But I'm not talking," Orville whispered.

"Right," Agatha answered. She began walking toward the school doors, and Orville followed.

"Now I have a question," she went on. "What was with all those bizarro questions you asked Jack?"

"What do you mean?" Orville whispered.

"All the boyfriend stuff. I mean, are you attempting a Bottomless Lake version of *The Bachelor* or what?"

"I asked Jack the same question you asked Tina," Orville whispered. "You asked if she had a boyfriend."

"Well, yeah," Agatha replied. "But I didn't ask her if she wanted one or what kind she wanted. Why did you keep grilling him?"

Orville blinked a few times. Then he started

whispering again. "I wanted to find out his motive."

"But what would having a girlfriend—or *wanting* a girlfriend—have to do with setting a fire during half-time?" Agatha asked.

"I don't know," Orville replied. "That's why I wanted to find out his motive."

Agatha studied her best friend. He was clearly a little confused by this whole motive thing. She wasn't surprised—Orville rarely understood why anyone did anything. It really frustrated him sometimes, made him feel left out and weird, and Agatha wished she could help him with it more. It was just that people—they were hard to explain. Agatha considered herself a people person, and even *she* didn't understand her species half the time.

They were at the school doors, and Agatha knew Orville's dad would be picking him up any minute. She'd have to explain motives—and proper questioning techniques—later. Right now they had to move on.

"So listen, I had a lightbulb experience during detention," Agatha said. "There's a totally obvious suspect that we haven't even mentioned."

"I know," Orville whispered excitedly. "It's—"

"It's the person who planned the Placid halftime prank," Agatha finished for him.

For some reason, Orville let out a deep sigh.

"So we need to investigate. It shouldn't be hard to

find out who planned the Placid halftime prank, right? It will just take a little snooping around."

Orville stared at her blankly.

"I mean, everyone at school knows who was on *our* prank committee, right?" Agatha rushed on. "So everyone at Placid must know who was on their committee. Although I really just want the big cheese. The one who planned the prank in the first place."

"The Sharks' prank?" Orville asked.

"Of course, the Sharks' prank," Agatha said. "Because they normally come up with much better pranks than the stupid band-uniform thing. Remember last year when they launched that mini hot air balloon?"

"Yes," Orville answered.

"Well, there you go," Agatha said. "Their pranks are usually so cool. And this year's was lame. So maybe their *real* prank was to set the fire and make sure *we* were blamed for it! That would be the work of a true evil genius. I wonder who it was."

"I know," Orville whispered.

Agatha narrowed her eyes and studied him. "What do you mean, you know?"

"I know who planned their prank."

Wait, Agatha thought. Was that possible? Could Orville really be hooked into some inter-school gossip grapevine that she didn't know existed? "Who?" Agatha asked.

"I don't know his name."

"Well, then how do you know he did it?"

"It's logical to assume that the culprit broke into our school's band room and painted on the shark bites before the band arrived to change into their uniforms," Orville whispered. "I don't think the band members would have stood still while he painted on them. Would they?"

Agatha couldn't help smiling at the thought. "I doubt it."

"Well, then, I assume he broke in before the band arrived. And there is only one window into the band room. The windowsill is splintering." He closed his mouth and just stood there.

Agatha waited for some kind of explanation, but clearly Orville was done talking. "O-kay," she said slowly. "And why does the windowsill matter?"

"I saw him at the snack shack before the football game. He was picking splinters out of the palm of his hand. Plus he had three green pebbles stuck between the laces of his sneakers."

"Pebbles?" Agatha asked.

Orville nodded matter-of-factly. "The same green pebbles as those in the empty band room fish tank."

Agatha pictured the band room. The giant fish tank was right underneath the window. "You mean, he fell in when he climbed through the window?" she asked, starting to really believe that Orville might know what he was talking about.

"Yes," Orville whispered. "And he had speckles of red paint on the sleeve of his shirt."

"From painting on the red shark bites," Agatha said. "That's amazing. I can't believe you noticed all this stuff!"

Orville looked almost surprised. "Why not?" he asked. "I always notice things that you don't."

Agatha had to admit he had a point there. In fact, she was usually sort of overwhelmed by the amount of tiny, weird details that Orville noticed about people and things. It was one of the strange personality quirks that she always advised Orville to keep to himself. Because it was, well, weird. But apparently it was also incredibly useful when it came to solving crimes. "You've convinced me," she told him. "So who is this guy?"

"I don't know his name," Orville repeated.

"All right," Agatha said patiently. "Then tell me what he looks like. Maybe *I* know his name."

"Okay," Orville whispered. "He's sixty-six inches tall, with an additional one inch of hair that stands straight up."

"What color hair? Platinum, auburn, strawberry, sable, chestnut?"

Agatha thought she could see Orville's eyes beginning to twirl. "Let's start at the beginning. Red, brown, blond, black. Which of those four?"

"Brown," he finally decided.

"Light or dark brown?"

He seemed stumped by the question.

"Your brown or my brown?" Agatha asked. Her own hair was almost black, while Orville's had golden highlights in it.

"Neither," he whispered. "It's his own color."

"Never mind," Agatha said. "What about his eyes?"

"The overhead lighting prevented me from seeing his eye color accurately," Orville reported. "I noticed that one eye appeared green while the other looked brown. I've never seen that before."

"Maybe they're hazel." Agatha sighed. So far all she really knew about this mystery guy was that his hair stood straight up. That could be a hundred different guys from Placid. Who would've thought just getting an accurate description of him would be the hardest part?

"His sneakers were a size ten," Orville added helpfully. "His feet were out of proportion to his body. I estimated that his feet made up fifteen percent of his total body weight."

"Really?" Agatha asked. "Then he must be pretty skinny."

"Yes," Orville whispered.

"What was he wearing?" Agatha asked in desperation.

Orville shrugged. He *really* didn't care about clothes.

"Can you remember anything else about him?"

"He smelled like a mixture of deer dung and brine shrimp."

Agatha took a moment to digest that little fact. "Huh?" she said.

"His odor was quite strong. No one else stood within twenty inches of him, even though the average space between people in the snack shack was eleven inches."

Agatha grinned. Now they were getting somewhere! "So he reeked," she said.

Orville didn't answer.

"Deer poop and shrimp." Who did she know who could possibly smell like that? "Are you sure that's what it was?"

"No," Orville replied. "Those were my best estimates of the two main odors. I was trying to get a closer sniff when the fight broke out and he moved away."

"Wait a minute," Agatha said. "He was in that fight? The one that Stu started?"

"Yes," Orville whispered. "He defended Samantha."

"Orville!" Agatha cried. "Why didn't you say so?"

Orville shrugged again. "Why does it matter?"

"Because there were only three or four people involved in that fight." She thought back to the snack shack. Stu had insulted Samantha. Then some of her friends had yelled at him. First Chet. But his hair was bleached blond. And then the girl with brown hair in the multi-buns had gotten in Stu's grill. But she was a girl. Orville had that distinction down. And then there was . . .

"Richie Cruz!" Agatha said aloud. "He totally stinks of aftershave! He's been wearing it since third grade 'cause he thinks it makes him cool and mature!"

"Is there deer dung in aftershave?" Orville asked.

"Who knows?" Agatha said. "Orville, you're a genius!"

"Yes," he confirmed. "I am."

Agatha smiled. Orville never lied, even to be modest. "So you knew all along who did the Sharks' prank," she said. "Why didn't you mention it to me?"

"I didn't know you were interested in that," Orville whispered. "I thought we were looking for the person who set the fire."

"But the person who planned the Sharks' prank might also be the person who set the fire," Agatha explained.

Orville cocked his head. "But what would be the motive?"

"The motive? To pull a really big prank on us. To make our school get blamed for burning the field."

"Why?" Orville asked.

"To get us in trouble."

"Why?"

Agatha hesitated. Was there a way to explain this kind of thing to Orville? "Because they're spiteful," she said.

"What is their motive for being spiteful?"

"It's not a good motive. It's not reasonable or logical or nice," Agatha admitted. "I think the Sharks don't like us and we don't like them. For some people, that's enough."

"So the kind of person you are determines the kind of motives you have," Orville said.

"Yeah. But there are no rules for this stuff, Orville.

It's just people, remember. We make no sense," Agatha told him. "Come on. We need to question our new suspect. And I know just where to find him."

"Where?"

"At the arcade in the mall. My cousin Eleanor worked there for about two seconds once. She said Richie hung out there all the time. She quit because he stank up the whole place."

The arcade at the Albert L. Placid Mall was always packed on Saturdays. But on weekdays, only the hardcore gamers showed up. Agatha crossed her fingers, hoping that Richie Cruz was still as into video games as he used to be.

The place was pretty empty, the machines just making their little pre-programmed noises. Would Richie even be here?

Orville whispered something to her, but Agatha couldn't hear him over the noise of the machines. "What?" she asked loudly. "Whisper in my ear."

Orville recoiled as if she might bite him. Agatha sighed. Orville hated to be touched so much that he wouldn't even get close enough for touching to be possible. "Well, I can't hear you if you won't talk in my ear," she complained.

Orville pointed to a little alcove in the back of the arcade. It was filled with the big, bulky old-fashioned games that Agatha hated. But it was also filled with a small crowd of Placid guys. They stood gathered around the Space Invaders game, watching Richie Cruz at the controls. "There's our prankster," Agatha told Orville. She strode quickly toward the crowd

"Grab some air, Cruz," she said when they reached the alcove. She couldn't resist. It was one of her favorite lines from *Badge of Bravery*.

Richie didn't put his hands up like the suspect in the novel, but he did turn, surprised. On the video game screen, a space invader landed on Richie's player. All the guys watching gasped in horror. Too late, Richie spun back around to begin playing. But another space invader hit him and that was the end of Richie.

"Game over," Agatha said, feeling pleased with herself. She had Cruz off balance, just like she wanted him.

"That was really rude," Richie grumbled. "Why didn't you let me finish my game?"

"Yeah," chorused the other guys. Agatha noticed that they were all skinny, dweeby, and no older than her.

"It's true," Orville whispered. "My social skills teacher says that interrupting is always rude."

Richie snickered. "See, even Retardo here agrees."

"That's it!" Agatha snapped. She took two fast steps toward her suspect, backing Richie up against the video game. "Hey," he protested, his eyes widening in fear.

"The rest of you get lost!" Agatha commanded in

what she hoped was a tough voice. To her astonishment, they actually did, disappearing out into the main arcade as fast as their scrawny legs would carry them.

"You guys—wait!" Richie called plaintively, but the dweebs were gone.

"Looks like you got some fair-weather friends," Agatha said. Her auntie Susan said this whenever Agatha complained about someone at school.

"Your voice is twelve percent more guttural than usual," Orville informed her in a whisper.

Agatha felt her cheeks heat up. He was going to blow her tough-guy image! "How can you possibly tell what percentage my voice is different?" she asked in her normal voice.

Orville took a deep breath, obviously ready to launch into some long and detailed scientific explanation.

"Never mind," Agatha said hastily. She turned back to Richie. He was wearing an expression that she'd named just for Stu in third grade: yellow-bellied-marmot-spotted-by-owl. Richie looked ready to bolt. For an eighth grader, he was a real baby.

"What do you want?" he asked. "I'm gonna call mall security."

"We know you planned the Placid prank," Agatha told him.

"No, I didn't."

"Yes, you did!" She leaned in close, hoping to bring

herself eye to eye with him. But even though he was skinny, Richie was almost a foot taller than Agatha. She found herself staring at his gigantic Adam's apple. She quickly pulled back. "Orville has proof."

"No, I don't," Orville whispered.

Agatha sighed. "Okay, maybe you don't *have* proof," she admitted. "But you *saw* evidence on Richie's person that proved he was completely guilty of prank planning. Tell him what you saw on the day of the football game."

"You had splinters in your hand, three green pebbles in your shoelaces, and roughly twelve speckles of red paint on your shirt," Orville told Richie. He used his normal voice, since Ms. Winogrand hadn't ordered him not to talk to Richie Cruz.

"See?" Agatha said.

Now Richie just looked baffled. "That doesn't prove anything!" he sputtered.

"Look, Cruz, we know you did it. Why are you trying to lie about it?" Agatha said. "In our school, the prank planners are proud of their work."

Richie puffed himself up a little. "Okay, fine," he said. "I did pull the prank."

"All by yourself?" Agatha asked.

"No. I had three helpers," Richie said. "But I'm the one who planned it."

Agatha grinned. Now she had him singing like a canary! "Well, you should be ashamed of yourself, Richie," she said. "Because your prank was incredibly lame!"

For the first time Richie stood up straight. "It was not!"

Agatha couldn't believe her ears. "It was *so* lame," she shot back. "So incredibly lame that all the Monster fans just laughed. Shark bites on the band? Is that the best you could do?"

Richie pushed past her. "It was a good prank!" he yelled. "Those bites were cool!"

"As cool as blaming John Q. for burning down your field house?" Agatha demanded, following Richie as he stormed through the arcade. "As cool as getting us in trouble for ruining the football field?"

Richie stopped and turned to her, surprised. "What are you talking about?" he said. "I didn't get you blamed for anything."

"Your true prank was a lot more dastardly than just painting on some shark bites," Agatha told him. "Because you're diabolical, Richie, *and* you're an arsonist!"

Richie's mouth dropped open. "You're insane," he said.

"We have a videotape that shows the bleachers during halftime," Orville put in. "You're not on it."

To Agatha's great satisfaction, Richie's face turned white. They had him!

"Where were you during halftime, Cruz?" she asked. "Where were you when the field house fire started?"

Richie stared at them for a moment, his lips trembling. "I—it's none of your business. Just leave me alone!" he finally blurted. He turned and raced out of the arcade. In a minute he was out of sight, running down the hallway of the mall.

Agatha turned to Orville. "Sweet! Our suspect has absolutely no alibi. Orville, we are on our way to solving this case!"

When Agatha entered the shop later that afternoon, she found her three-year-old cousins, Nicky and Kate, yelling, screaming, and running circles around Nana's legs. Aunt Louise was at the far end of the store, stocking the Bottomless Lake mineral water display. "Want to help behind the counter, Aggie?" Nana Wong asked.

Agatha hated when people called her Aggie. Except for Nana. She was allowed. "No thanks," Agatha said. "I have homework."

"Okay, sweetie. Why don't you use the back room?" Nana said. "By the way, Darrell and his friends only broke one Trixie. And it wasn't even an expensive one. You owe me just $11.95."

"Wait. You're making me pay retail?" Agatha protested.

Nana waved her hand in dismissal. "Fine, fine. Make it five bucks even. Now go hit those books."

Agatha grabbed her backpack and lugged it into the storeroom. She did have homework, but that could wait until later. She had her *life* to think about first. She pulled her Spider-Man notebook out of her backpack and opened it to the suspects page. Tina Gore was crossed out, but there were two suspects without alibis for the time the fire was set: Richie Cruz and Jack Simmons.

It can't be Jack, she thought for the zillionth time. *He's no knight in shining armor, but he's basically a good guy.* The idea of Jack betraying his team—and his school—didn't make sense. Agatha decided to concentrate on Richie for now.

Richie had a motive—to play the meanest prank ever on the Monsters. His own confession proved that he'd painted the shark bites. Did he actually think that was a good prank? No way. So burning the field house had to be the real prank. Richie had no alibi for halftime during the fire. "But where's the evidence?" Agatha murmured. Among all the details Orville had noticed about Richie, none had linked him to the fire. Were they missing something?

Agatha sighed. What would a real investigator do next?

"Go to the tape!" she cried. Samantha's halftime videotape was still in her backpack. Maybe if she watched it again, she'd notice something she didn't see the first time. Maybe there was a frame or two of Richie walking near the field house.

Agatha rummaged around among the Trixie masks in the storage cabinet and found Nana's portable TV. It was a tiny little VCR-TV combo that hadn't worked properly ever since Cousin Eddie spilled grape juice on it two years ago. But Agatha was pretty sure the VCR part still worked. It was worth a try, anyway. She set it on a broken display counter, plugged it in, popped in Samantha's tape, and pressed play.

The screen sputtered to life. There was a dark bar along the bottom and apparently the TV only showed things in black and white, but Agatha could still see well enough. She sat down on a box of candy Trixie eggs and began to watch. Samantha was talking to the Placid kids in the bleachers. There was Richie Cruz sitting with his posse of dweebs off to the right. Agatha was sure they called themselves a "posse." Gag. It was such a dweeb-like thing to do.

Richie looked sort of embarrassed, Agatha thought. Every time Samantha came near him with the camera, he inched away. "As if she'd really ever interview him," Agatha said. Even when Richie had come to Samantha's defense in the snack shack, Samantha had pretty much ignored him.

Soon enough the game started, and the tape mostly showed footage of the teams on the field until halftime. Agatha reached over to press fast forward, and the little football players sped across the field at double time. Agatha cringed as she noticed Jack's pass to the Sharks' receiver. It was officially called an interception, but there weren't even any Monster players near the guy— and Jack had thrown the ball straight to him.

Wait. Agatha hit pause. *Were* there other Monsters

nearby? She squinted at the small screen. There were two other players within a few yards of the Shark receiver. But were they Sharks or Monsters? She couldn't tell. On the black-and-white TV, the uniforms all looked the same.

Agatha thought back to the game. Samantha had been doing a piece on the Sharks' new uniforms, which introduced a new scheme. The Sharks' colors had always been red and white, but their new uniforms were red with green numbers. Lissa had made that comment to Sam about the Sharks being unoriginal. At the time, Agatha hadn't thought much about it. But now she realized how important the Sharks' new color was. She peered at the TV screen again. The reds and greens all just showed up as gray. The two teams looked almost identical in black and white.

Black and white.

Agatha leapt to her feet so suddenly that she knocked the box of candy eggs over onto its side. Watching the game in black and white . . . it was sort of like being color blind. And if a player—like, say, Jack—actually *was* color blind, that was how he would see the uniforms.

Agatha ran out into the shop. Nicky and Kate were out cold in the Trixie bedding aisle. Agatha shook her head. It was zero to sixty with those two. When they got tired, it was lights out!

"Nana!" Agatha cried.

"With a customer," Nana Wong replied cheerfully. She was in the middle of selling a matching Trixie necklace-and-earrings set to a middle-aged Latina lady. Agatha was too impatient to wait for the whole sales pitch. She rushed over to the woman and gave a big, excited gasp.

"Ohmigod, are you buying those?" she cried.

The lady smiled at her. "I'm thinking about it," she said. "My daughter just got her ears pierced and I want to bring her a souvenir. I always bring home a gift when I travel for business," she added, turning back to Nana Wong.

"How sweet," Nana cooed. "What line of business are you in?"

Agatha inserted herself between the two women. "Your daughter will *love* those," she gushed. "Every single girl at my school has that set. They're like a guarantee of popularity. You should really get them."

The lady gazed down at the jewelry in her hand. Agatha thought she looked pretty convinced. "Hey, Aunt Louise, can you ring this lady up?" she called to her aunt, who was now dusting the model of Bottomless Lake that sat in the front window. "I need to talk to Nana."

"Oh, well . . ." The customer seemed surprised.

"Your daughter will be so psyched!" Agatha told her, doing her best to sound like a cheerleader. Then she grabbed Nana's arm and dragged her into the back room.

"Aggie, I've told you not to interrupt me with a customer," Nana began in her lecturing tone of voice.

"I know, I'm sorry," Agatha said in a rush. "Didn't you tell me that Uncle Richard is color blind?"

Nana Wong narrowed her eyes. "Excuse me?"

"It's important," Agatha assured her.

"Is this about that fire?"

"Yes! I had a breakthrough," Agatha said. "I think."

"And what does your uncle Richard have to do with it?"

"Nothing. But I think you said he has a certain kind of color blindness. What is it?"

"He has red-green color blindness," Nana Wong said. "It's very common in males."

"I knew it!" Agatha pumped her fist in the air. "So red looks like green and green looks like red, right?"

"Right," Nana said. "Or at least red and green look the same to him. I don't know if either one looks like what we think of as red or green." She planted her hands on her hips. "Now, Agatha Eugenia Wong, what's this all about?"

"Jack!" Agatha said. "During the football game on Saturday, he seemed all confused. He even passed the ball to the wrong team. But all the uniforms are red and green."

"So you think this Jack boy is color blind?" Nana asked.

"Yeah. Poor Jack." Agatha felt a rush of sympathy for him. "He must've been so baffled out on the field. Thanks to him, our team was losing really bad."

"Really?" Nana cocked an eyebrow. "Didn't you tell me the game was stopped after that fire broke out?"

"Yeah."

"Well, then it seems to me that your Jack had a pretty good reason for wanting the game to be called off," Nana said. "If the game was canceled, he wouldn't be able to make any more bad plays. Now, if you'll excuse me, I think I'll check on that customer you did such a good sales job on."

Nana Wong went back to work and Agatha returned to the TV in the storeroom. The tape was paused, and all the uniforms looked the same. She stared at the image of Jack on the field. He was so graceful and strong. But Nana Wong was right. Jack had been making a fool of himself on Saturday. Samantha had even joked about it during her commentary. Plus he'd been losing the big game for his team.

"After the fire, the game ended," Agatha said sadly. "And no one has even mentioned Jack's bad playing since then."

She couldn't deny it. Jack had a motive.

Jack Simmons could definitely be the arsonist.

Chapter 7

The phone rang two minutes after dinner. Orville knew there was an eighty-seven percent chance that it was Agatha. She knew exactly what time he ate every evening, just like she knew exactly what food he ate: a grilled chicken breast with nothing on it and five tablespoons of creamed corn, followed by four Doublestuf Oreos. It took Orville 10.3 minutes to eat his dinner. Agatha was one of the few people who could calculate what time he would be finished and ready to talk on the phone.

But he wasn't allowed to talk to her. What if he answered the phone in a whisper and it wasn't Agatha? Miss Eloise had spent four entire social skills classes on what to do when the phone rang. Orville had memorized the process: One, you couldn't ignore it no matter how focused you were on what you were doing. Two, you couldn't just pick up the phone and wait for the other person to talk. You had to speak in a loud, clear voice and say "hello" or "the Wright residence." Agatha had told him to use "hello," so that was what he usually did. But if he said "hello" into the phone in his normal voice and it turned out to be Agatha on the other end, would that be violating Ms. Winogrand's rule?

"Orville!" his mom said, breaking into his thoughts. "It's Agatha."

Orville looked up at his mother. He hadn't noticed her answering the phone. "Thank you," he told her, just like Miss Eloise had taught him. He took the phone. "Hello?" he whispered.

"Orville? I can't hear you," Agatha said.

"I'm whispering," he whispered.

"Well, that's gonna be hard to hear on the phone. Maybe you can mumble?" Agatha suggested.

"I will *siiiiing*," Orville sang.

"Good. Listen, I've been going over our suspect notes."

Orville saw no need to reply to that, so he didn't.

"We have two people without alibis for the time the fire was set," Agatha went on. "Jack and Richie."

Still Orville didn't see the need to say anything.

"So we need to investigate them both. I think we should split up."

There was a pause. Agatha seemed to be waiting for an answer. Orville knew that if a pause in conversation lasted longer than four seconds, it usually meant that the other person expected him to say something. "*Okaaaaaay*," he sang. He found that that was generally what the other person wanted him to say.

"Great," Agatha said. "So I'm going to talk some more to Jack." Her voice became higher pitched, as it usually did when she mentioned Jack's name. "Do you think you can try to find Richie Cruz again? My cousin said Richie spends half his life at the arcade."

"I'll go there *toooo-niiiiiight*," Orville sang.

"Great. Really grill him for an alibi," Agatha said. "And take a good, close look at him. Maybe you'll spot some evidence that links him to the fire."

There was another pause. Orville counted the seconds. One . . . two . . . three . . . four.

"*Okaaaaaay*," he sang.

"Usually I wouldn't want you going to the mall this late," Orville's father said as he backed out of the driveway. "But with Esther and Jeremy here in need of a ride, it's your lucky night."

Orville glanced at the two pigs in the backseat. Their names weren't really Esther and Jeremy. Their names were Pig #3 and Pig #5. There were six pigs involved in the Esther and Jeremy Show at The Grotto, even though there were officially only two famous swimming pigs. But Orville's dad called all the sows Esther and all the boars Jeremy. Esther after Esther Williams, an actress who swam in all her movies, and Jeremy after Olympic gold medal swimmer Jeremy Linn.

"Where are you taking them?" Orville asked.

"Back to their sty," his father said cheerfully. "I worked with them for three hours this afternoon on a new trick. I'm going to try it out at the show tomorrow."

Orville thought about that. His father was the trainer for all the swimming pigs. But he couldn't teach them new tricks at the lake. If he did, the tourists might see, and the pigs were supposed to be natural swimmers, at least according to the restaurant's owner. So whenever Mr. Wright trained the pigs to do anything new, he brought them home and taught them in the family swimming pool.

"What's the trick?" Orville asked.

"I've got Esther doing somersaults while Jeremy swims in a circle around her," his dad told him. "It's hilarious."

Pig #3 snorted. The pigs snorted an average of twelve percent more frequently when riding in the car than they did when they were in their sty or in the Wright backyard.

Orville considered the goal Agatha had given him— find Richie Cruz and gather more evidence. It seemed like a straightforward task. While he was doing that, perhaps he could also find out more about motive—and figure out the motive of the person he knew set the fire, The One Who Is Innocent Until Proven Guilty.

"Dad, why did you teach Esther and Jeremy that trick?" Orville asked.

His dad smiled. "I told you, it's hilarious," he said.

"Was that your *motive* for teaching the pigs a new trick?" Orville pressed.

Now his father seemed confused. Orville knew that

when Mr. Wright blinked several times in a row, it indicated confusion. "Well, I don't know if that was my *motive*," he said. "I guess I just thought it might be fun."

"So you don't know what your motive was?"

"No. I'm not sure I do."

Maybe not understanding motives runs in my family, Orville thought. Did that mean he'd never understand them? Or just that it would be incredibly difficult? His father stopped the car in front of the main mall entrance.

"It will take me about half an hour to get the pigs back to the restaurant and settle them in their sty," Mr. Wright told him. "Then I'll pick you up on the way home. So be right back here in thirty-five minutes, okay?"

"Okay." Thirty-five minutes should be enough time to search for evidence linking The One Who Is Innocent Until Proven Guilty to the fire.

Orville climbed out of the car and headed into the mall. He turned right at the first hall and headed straight for the arcade. Agatha wanted him to question Richie Cruz, so that was what he would do. He wasn't really sure what he was supposed to ask, other than what they had already asked Richie this afternoon. But Agatha seemed to think that further questioning would cause Richie to give different answers. Maybe he should phrase the questions differently? He planned out several variations of the question "Where were you when the fire started?" on the walk to the arcade.

Inside the arcade, it was even emptier than it had been this afternoon. Two older girls were standing near the front counter with a boy who wore an Albert's Arcade apron. And ten feet inside was . . . not Richie, but Stu Frysley. He was playing the game where you had to dance along, doing the moves that the machine told you as fast as you could. Stu looked like he was performing some sort of Native American tribal ritual.

Meet eye, say hi. Miss Eloise's instructions echoed in Orville's mind. He approached Stu. He couldn't meet Stu's eyes because Stu was staring at his feet. Orville wasn't sure how to deal with this. He cleared his throat and said, "Hi."

Stu leapt off the dancing mat. His cheeks, neck, and ears turned bright red. "What are you doing here, loser?" he snapped.

Orville thought back to Miss Eloise's class on greetings. Stu's greeting hadn't been mentioned. Maybe that meant it didn't require an answer. He stepped past Stu and kept walking toward the back of the arcade.

"So how's your investigation going?" Stu called after him. "Did the Rejected Detectives find anything yet?"

The loud, rasping sound coming from Stu's throat was probably laughter, Orville decided. Stu hadn't paused before laughing, so Orville concluded that he wasn't waiting for an answer to his questions. But since they were having a conversation, Orville decided to try figuring out a motive for Stu's strange behavior.

"Why do you always smell like Swiss cheese?" he asked.

Stu stopped laughing. He shot a glance at the two girls near the arcade worker. "Shut up, freak," he whispered.

Orville counted to four. "Okay," he said. He turned and headed to the back of the arcade, where he and Agatha had spoken to Richie earlier. The problem was, Richie wasn't there. In fact, nobody was there except for one forty-nine-inch-tall girl with a temporary tattoo peeling off her right forearm. She was playing Space Invaders, the game Richie had played earlier. She smelled like cinnamon buns from the mall food court.

Orville studied her hands on the control sticks. Her ring finger bowed out about four millimeters to the left. It had obviously been broken at one point. He glanced at her hair. There was a cowlick on the upper-right quadrant of her skull. He looked at her feet. They were extremely large. He estimated that they made up nine percent of her body weight.

This girl was clearly related to big-footed Richie Cruz.

The sounds from the video game indicated that her game was over. The girl smiled as the top scores list popped up on-screen. At the top of the list—in the top five slots—were the initials R.C.C. The number 1 was blinking. The girl typed in her initials—R.G.C.

That settled it. This girl was Richie's sister, Orville decided. He supposed she could be a cousin, but sister seemed statistically more likely. Agatha was the only person he knew who had cousins that lived in the same town as her.

I have to question her, Orville thought. Since Richie wasn't here, his sister would be the next-best thing. Maybe she would have information that Richie hadn't told them. Orville's palms became moist with sweat and his heart rate increased. That meant he was nervous. He didn't like talking to strangers, at least not without Agatha.

Miss Eloise had taught his social skills class about approaching strangers for a conversation. First you had to introduce yourself. As the girl went over to the change machine to buy some more tokens, Orville ran through Miss Eloise's instructions in his mind: Offer a compliment or an observation to get the conversation started. Make eye contact, extend your hand to shake, say hello, and tell the other person what your name is.

The girl turned in his direction, so Orville stepped up to her, making sure to look her in the eyes. Now he needed a compliment. His mind was a total blank.

"You played Space Invaders," he said. That wasn't a compliment, was it?

"You bet I did!" she cried.

Orville extended his hand, ready to introduce himself. But the girl just kept on talking. "I beat the top score, did you see that? I can beat every top score in this place. I'm the king of the arcade."

Was he supposed to say something now? Orville began

counting the seconds. The girl started talking again after 2.3. "I'm halfway through the back room," she said. "I have to finish all the games here before my mom gets done shopping. But it's no problem—I can do it. I totally rule."

"Why do you want to play every game?" Orville asked. "What's your motive?"

"To humiliate my brother," the girl said. "Duh." She dropped some tokens in the Centipede game and began playing.

"Your brother is Richie," Orville told her.

"Yeah, do you know him? Don't you think he'll be, like, crushed when he sees my name on top of all of his scores?"

"What is your name?" Orville asked.

"Rachel Cruz. Otherwise known as Rachel the great. I used to make Richie call me that. And he was Richie the all-powerful."

"How come you can beat his scores?" Orville asked. "Isn't all-powerful better than great?"

Rachel snorted. "He's not really all-powerful. He's incredibly lame. He's Richie the all-lame."

"Why are you trying to humiliate him?" Orville asked.

"Because he keeps ignoring me," Rachel said. "He's in eighth grade now, so that means he's the oldest in the school. Next year he'll be in high school. I guess that makes him too cool to hang out with his little sister anymore."

"But he used to hang out with you a lot?"

"All the time. He let me help with all his stuff, the science fairs and the Web design and all the prank plans. But now he's *embarrassed*."

"The prank plans?" Orville repeated. "You mean for the Monsters-Sharks games?"

Rachel shot him a look. "You mean the *Sharks*-Monsters games," she said. "Yeah. Remember that little balloon that launched from the top of the goalpost last year? That was my idea."

"That was an impressive prank," Orville said. "It took me almost six minutes to figure out how it was done."

"Of course it was impressive—I planned it," Rachel said. "Richie got all the credit, because I'm not sup-posed to use hazardous substances in my experiments." She rolled her eyes. "As if hydrogen is really hazardous. Please. But I let everyone think that Richie did it so my parents wouldn't find out. All he actually did was climb the goalpost to set it up."

"You are exceptionally intelligent," Orville told her.

"Obviously," Rachel said. "And Richie's the village idiot. Did you see that prank he pulled this year?"

"It was unimpressive."

"No kidding. That's what he comes up with when I don't help him!"

"Richie thought his prank was cool," Orville said. "He told me so."

Rachel's game of Centipede ended, and she put her initials over her brother's. "He did not—he knew it was the worst prank in history," she said. "He couldn't even stand to watch it. He came home before halftime even started because he was afraid everyone would boo him when they saw his stupid prank."

Orville thought about that. Richie was at home during halftime? That meant he could not have been at the field house starting the fire. It was an alibi—exactly what Agatha had wanted him to find out.

"Did you see Richie at home?" he asked Rachel.

"Of course. My parents wouldn't let me go to the game without him, and he said he didn't want me tagging along. I had to spend the whole day at home. But I got to make fun of him for hiding in his room instead of watching the prank." Rachel moved on to Ms. Pac-Man.

Orville had accomplished what Agatha sent him for. He began to walk away. Then he remembered something else Miss Eloise had taught them. "Good-bye," he called to Rachel. She ignored him.

Satisfied, Orville headed back out into the mall. He had eleven minutes left before he had to meet his dad. Time to do some more research about motives so that he could finally accuse The One Who Is Innocent Until Proven Guilty.

Suddenly a hand grabbed his arm—a blatant violation of the no-touching zone. Orville froze. He looked up to see Samantha Boutry standing less than a foot away. She wouldn't let go of his forearm.

"Hey!" she said. "Didn't you hear me calling you?"

An alarm screamed in Orville's head. He hated to be touched! Trying hard to control his panic, he took a step back and swallowed, and Samantha's hand slipped away from him. "No," he said.

"You were really off in your own world," Samantha commented. She glanced around the mall. The only other people in sight were a security guard and two women pushing baby strollers. It was almost time for the mall to close. "So what are you doing here? Still trying to clear your name?" Samantha asked.

"Agatha sent me to question one of her suspects," he told her.

Samantha raised her eyebrows. "Wow, you guys are really serious." She glanced around the hallway again. "Are you leaving now? I'll walk with you to the door." She slipped her arm through his and began walking back toward the food court. Orville had to follow—she was practically dragging him. His arm was trapped in hers! Alarm bells sounded in his head again, drowning out all his thoughts except one: he had to find a way to get Samantha to let go!

"Who was the suspect you questioned?" she asked as they walked.

"Rachel Cruz," Orville said. He tried to tug away, but Samantha held tight.

"Never heard of her." Samantha frowned. As they rounded the corner into the food court, she slowed down. "Hey! Want to see what I got?" she asked.

Maybe if I say yes, she'll let go of me, Orville thought. "Yes," he said.

"It's so cool." Samantha dropped his arm (whew!) and used both hands to open the white plastic bag she carried. Orville glanced down. There was a purple smear on his sleeve. Samantha must have gotten ink on him. "It's a whole manicure set. Check this out," she was saying. She held up a small box with a clear cover. Inside were several different nail files and clippers, all with matching handles made of some kind of sparkly pink plastic. "I lost one piece of the last set," Samantha explained, "but I like this one better anyway."

Orville began to breathe more quickly. His heart thudded in his chest. He looked at the nail stuff. Was he supposed to say something? He didn't think so. Samantha had never talked this much to him before. He didn't like it. He wished Agatha were here. She would have stopped Samantha from touching him.

"And then I got three different colors of nail polish because I always have to have something new, you know? People count on me to know what's gonna be hot next. Oh, and look, this is the best part!" Samantha held up a piece of cardboard with several tiny gold and silver fig-ures stuck to it. "It's nail jewelry!" she cried. "When you give yourself a manicure, you just peel off the backs and then they're all sticky. They stay on for days."

She paused. Orville counted the seconds. When he got to five, he opened his mouth to answer her . . . but he had no idea what to say. "Okay," he tried.

Samantha frowned. "They're more than okay," she said. Then she smiled again. "It will be a whole new trend!" She glanced around the almost-empty food court. "Let's go ask for free leftovers," she cried, reaching for his arm again. Orville hastily took a step back. Why did she keep trying to touch him?

"C'mon," Samantha said. Orville watched her hand coming closer . . . closer. She was an inch away from slipping her arm through his.

"Yaaaaah!" he screamed. He bolted for the door.

Chapter 8

"Thursday a.m.," Agatha muttered to herself as she wrote on a fresh page in her Spider-Man notebook. "Outside boys' locker room. Further investigation of Jack Simmons, suspect." She paused, lifting her pen from the paper as she glanced around. No one was in sight.

After finding out from Cousin Billy's best friend—who was the team manager—that the coach had called a special Sea Monsters team meeting this morning, Agatha had felt like a real detective with her finger on the pulse of the middle school. But here she was, loitering outside the locker room. And no one else had shown.

Agatha sighed. She was trying to feel hard-boiled. That's what Nana Wong said detectives were supposed to be. The only hard-boiled thing Agatha had ever seen was an egg, and she had a feeling that wasn't what Nana meant.

Agatha knew that when it came time to actually talk to Jack, she'd be feeling more *soft*-boiled than anything else. So she'd decided to snoop around a little first. She'd question Jack's teammates, and then she'd work up to questioning him.

Maybe one of the other football players will tell me

that Jack has a rock-solid alibi, Agatha thought. *Then I'll* never *have to question him again*. Of course, the first thing she had to do was convince one of the football players to actually talk to her—Leper Agatha.

She flipped her notebook shut and slid down the wall until she was sitting cross-legged on the tile floor. She should've known the players would all show up at the last minute. She was so early that even Coach Pettit wasn't here yet.

Agatha didn't want to believe that Jack could be their fire starter. But she had to face facts: he was the only suspect left. Tina Gore had an alibi, and according to Orville, Richie Cruz had an alibi too. Orville had called her last night with the news. Richie had been at home during halftime. That left Jack and only Jack. No matter how cute he was or how semi-nice he had been to her and Orville.

The sudden thud of footsteps filled the hall. Agatha leapt to her feet and put on her toughest, don't-mess-with-me face. She called it "rhino-poked-with-poker."

Kenneth Marshall and his younger brother, Kevin, pounded down the corridor toward the locker room. Everyone at school knew the Marshall brothers— Kenneth was the kicker on the team and his "little" brother Kevin was the biggest linebacker in the league, even though he was only a sixth grader.

Could have been a lot worse than these two slabs of meat, Agatha thought. Agatha had once beaten Kenneth up when he cut in front of her in the elementary school lunch line. Ever since then, he'd had a healthy respect for her. She knew she could make him tell her what she needed to know.

"Good to see you, Agatha," Kevin muttered. "The team's wanted you for a human sacrifice."

"Hold on a minute, boys," she said as Kevin reached for the locker room door. "I need to talk to you."

"We're late," Kenneth told her. "Coach said to be here at seven forty-five *sharp*."

"Well, Coach is just gonna have to cool his jets," Agatha said sternly.

"No way." Kevin pulled open the door. "We don't mess with the boss."

Kenneth looked a little worried at the idea of crossing Agatha. "Can we talk to you later?" he asked.

Agatha rolled her eyes. So much for being scary. "You guys, Coach Pettit isn't even here yet," she said. "You're the first to arrive."

The brothers exchanged a glance. "Seriously?" Kenneth asked.

"I told you we didn't need to run all the way to school," Kevin told his brother. He glanced at Agatha. "Still, we're not talking to her." They both turned toward the locker room.

"Oh, does big Kenny have to do everything little Kevvy tells him?" Agatha cooed.

"No," Kenneth said.

"Yes," Kevin said.

Instantly the brothers forgot about going into the locker room. They faced off against each other. Agatha smiled, satisfied. The things she'd learned from babysitting her cousins!

"So listen, before you go all Rock 'Em Sock 'Em Robots," Agatha interrupted. "You know how our prank committee got blamed for starting the fire last weekend?"

"You mean how you and Orville burned down the field house?" Kevin demanded, turning his wrath from Kenneth to her.

"Yeah, we know, Agatha," Kenneth told her. "We're turning in our uniforms today. That's what the meeting's for."

With two hundred pounds of Marshalls now staring at her, Agatha felt a tad uneasy. "Listen, you guys know Orville. He says it wasn't the prank that caused the fire. Orville never, ever lies."

Kenneth and Kevin grumbled an agreement. Everyone who knew Orville could tell he was incapable of lying.

"I think Jack Simmons started it," she blurted.

Now the brothers stared at her as if she'd lost her

mind. *"Jack?"* Kenneth cried. "That's crazy! He's the team captain!"

"I know," Agatha said. "But he has a motive. Remember how bad he was playing during that game?"

Kevin looked down at his feet. "He would've pulled it together in the second half," he muttered.

"Yeah," Kenneth put in. "And besides, everybody has a bad game now and then. It doesn't mean Jack went and set the field house on fire."

"Well, to me it seems like a motive. He didn't want to humiliate himself in the second half, so he made sure there was no second half," Agatha said. "And then there's the little matter of him having no alibi for the time of the fire. So I'm hoping you guys can fill me in. Where was Jack during halftime?"

Both Marshall boys turned pale. *That's not good*, Agatha thought, her heart tumbling. "Wasn't the team together in the locker room?" she pressed.

"Well, we're supposed run off the field and go straight to the locker room," Kevin said. "Then Coach gives us his talk, we chill for a while, and get ourselves ready for the second half."

Kenneth nodded in agreement. "When we've had a bad first half, it's especially important that we get back there fast because Coach will have a lot of talking to do. He analyzes what went wrong and tells us how to fix it when we go back out there."

"At that last game, a lot had gone wrong," Kevin admitted. "Coach was really, uh, anxious to start discussing it."

"So what happened?" Agatha asked, resisting the urge to plug her ears and do the la-la-la thing.

"We never got the talk," Kevin said. "Coach Pettit didn't want to start without Jack, especially because Jack was the one messing up the most that day. But Jack wasn't there."

"Where was he?"

The Marshall brothers shrugged. "Nobody knew," Kenneth told her. "He was with us when we left the field. But when we got back to the locker room, he just wasn't there. We all figured he went off somewhere to get his head together."

"He was pretty bummed about his bad game," Kevin put in.

"So we were all waiting for him to show up so that Coach could start," Kenneth went on.

"And then what happened?" Agatha asked.

"The fire started out on the field," Kenneth said. "We heard the alarms and people yelling, and then Coach got on the walkie-talkie and found out what was happening. He told us all to clear out because the game was canceled. Then he ran out to the field to help."

"And you never saw Jack," Agatha said sadly.

The Marshalls shook their heads, but they didn't say a word. Agatha knew they were thinking the same thing she was: Jack had no alibi.

And he was looking guiltier and guiltier by the minute.

By the time detention rolled around, Agatha had gotten over feeling sad about Jack. The more she thought about it, the more obviously guilty he seemed. He had been making a fool of himself and his team—a perfect motive. He knew all about their prank and he knew exactly when the Trixie fire would start—a perfect opportunity. He was AWOL when the fire started—no alibi. Now she just needed some evidence. And she was in no mood to spend a lot of time looking for it. Jack had already caused enough trouble for her and Orville. And pretending to be nice to them didn't make up for it! She was going to see to it that they didn't spend one more day in the pen because of something he had done. She was going to see to it that Lissa got to be president again. She was going to see to it that she and Orville were returned to the status of human beings! And she was going to see to it today!

She stomped into Ms. Winogrand's room, wishing she was wearing her boots. When you were going to kick some booty, you should be wearing boots. But her pink sneaks would have to do. She sat down right next to Jack and glared at him. *He is not cute,* she told herself sternly. *He's a criminal. And crime is ugly.*

Ms. Winogrand peered around the room suspiciously. Finally she turned her accusing frown on Agatha. "Where is your friend Orville?" she demanded. "Did he sneak out again?"

Agatha turned off her angry-gorilla-on-steroids look and put on her noble-yet-helpful-rescue-dog smile for the teacher. "He's excused from detention today. You were supposed to get a note from Principal Rothman," she explained. "Orville has his social skills class on Thursdays."

From behind her, she heard Stu give a loud snort. "Too bad he's never learned anything there," he joked.

Agatha turned her mean look back on and spun toward Stu. "You're just jealous that they don't give classes for morons," she told him.

"That's enough!" Ms. Winogrand was trying to sound strict, but Agatha could tell she was confused. She shuffled the papers on her desk, looking for the principal's note about Orville. Agatha knew it must be there somewhere—Orville's mom was just as organized and thorough as Orville was.

With the teacher distracted, Agatha turned her attention to Jack. She quickly pushed her desk closer to his. She didn't want Stu eavesdropping on their conversation. Jack looked surprised to see her so close.

"You're not gonna start interrogating me again, are you?" he said.

"Nope," Agatha told him. "I don't need to because I already know you did it." It was amazing how much easier it was to talk to him now that she had some righteous anger on her side.

"What? You're crazy," Jack said.

"And you're color blind," Agatha retorted.

Jack's head swiveled toward her. His eyes were wide. "What are you talking about?" he demanded.

"The game on Saturday. You were totally messing up. You couldn't tell which team was which."

"I had a bad game," Jack said. "Don't you think I'm embarrassed enough already? Why do you have to keep talking about it?"

"You had such a bad game that you were going to be blamed for a big, big loss to the Sharks," Agatha told him. "I think you couldn't stand the idea of having to do the Walk of Shame around school."

"Look, everyone plays badly sometimes," Jack protested. "I just wish the football field was going to be usable again so that I could prove how good I am."

"But you knew the field would be ruined by the fire," Agatha said. "So the season would be canceled. And after this season, you'll be in high school. You won't care about the Monsters at all anymore."

Jack heaved a sigh. "Why would I want to ruin my

last chance at playing for the Monsters? I was the starting quarterback this year!"

"But if Coach Pettit found out that you're color blind, he might worry that you'd keep playing badly," Agatha said. "And then he wouldn't recommend you for the junior varsity team at the high school. So you figured out a way he'd never have to know."

"You're right, okay?" Jack exploded. "You're totally right. I'm color blind, and I couldn't tell the two teams apart, and I was worried that Coach would think I couldn't play because of it."

Cracked you like an egg, Agatha thought. "So you snuck over to the field house during halftime, you waited until our prank started, and then you set the fire so it would look like the sparks from Trixie blew up the field house."

"No," Jack said. "I snuck into the equipment room during halftime and started putting tape on all my teammates' helmets. That way, I'd be able to tell them apart from the other team."

Agatha blinked. She hadn't been expecting that. "Tape?" she repeated.

"Yeah. A big piece of duct tape on the front of the helmet and another one around the back from one side to the other." Jack shrugged. "It was the only thing I could think of."

"That's kind of a good idea," Agatha said lamely.

"But it doesn't matter now. The season's over." Jack glanced at her with worried eyes. "You won't tell anyone, will you? About the color-blind thing? I hardly ever even notice it—it was just those new uniforms."

All of Agatha's anger melted away. And that meant that her ability to speak to Jack without sounding like a dope was also circling the drain. "No," she said.

He raised a questioning eyebrow.

"Um, I won't," Agatha added. "Tell."

"Cool." Jack smiled the all-powerful Jack Simmons smile.

Agatha grinned back at him, even though she wasn't quite sure what she was smiling for. Jack just had that effect on people. "You should, though," she told him.

"Should what?"

"Tell Coach Pettit you're color blind," Agatha suggested. "I mean, it's not like you're trying to be an astronaut."

Jack's brows knitted together in confusion.

"You know, where the color-blind thing matters," Agatha sputtered. "I mean, I don't think it keeps people from being football stars. Maybe the coach could help you."

"That's true," Jack said thoughtfully. "Maybe I will."

"Good." Agatha clamped her mouth shut. Jack understood what she meant. If she talked any more, she was sure to mess it up.

"So I'm off the hook, right?" he asked. "You know I'm not the arsonist?"

Agatha was just about to say yes when she realized that she hadn't even checked on Jack's alibi. She had been ready to take his word for it just because he was cute!

"Not exactly," she said. "I need to know if anyone saw you. You know, with the tape. And the helmets."

"Yeah. Nathan was helping me. I couldn't tape up the whole team in time all by myself."

Agatha glanced across the room. Nathan was sleeping with his head on his desk.

Then she took a look at Ms. Winogrand.

The detention monitor was engrossed in the horror novel hidden behind her lesson plan folder. But Agatha knew she'd notice if anyone moved. As quietly as she could, Agatha ripped a page from her Spider-Man notebook. She quickly wrote a note: *Nathan—Important! Where were you during halftime when the fire started?*

Would he tell her the same story as Jack?

Agatha folded the page into a small paper triangle and flicked it at Nathan. The sharp point hit him right on the cheek, and he sprang up as if he'd been slapped. His chair legs shrieked against the tile floor as he backed away from the desk.

Ms. Winogrand looked up, her eyes narrowed. Nathan gave her a little wave. They all sat still until the teacher frowned and went back to her book.

Agatha caught Nathan's eye and gestured to the note. He unfolded it, read it, and then shot a look at Jack.

After Jack gave him a nod, Nathan scribbled something on the paper, re-folded it, and flicked it back at her. Agatha read: *I was with Jack in the equipment room, but I can't tell you why.*

She gave him a thumbs-up. He didn't want to tell Jack's secret about the color blindness, but he'd told her exactly where they were. It matched Jack's story. That was the end of Jack as a suspect. He had a rock-solid alibi.

I thought I'd be happy about that, Agatha realized. *And I am. But now it means I have no suspects left!*

Faux pas. That's what Miss Eloise had written on the board. Orville didn't know those words, so he wrote them down in his marble-patterned notebook. Then he thought about The One Who Is Innocent Until Proven Guilty. He was no closer to figuring out a motive for The One than he had been on Monday. He'd asked a lot of people about their motives for doing a lot of things. And the only common factor among their answers had been that they didn't make sense. So how could he figure out a motive for The One Who Is Innocent Until Proven Guilty?

"Orville?" Miss Eloise's voice broke into his thoughts. She was standing right next to his desk. He got the feeling that she'd been there for a while. "You're concentrating on your own thoughts again, aren't you?" she asked.

"Yes," Orville admitted.

"Remember what we talked about?"

"Yes," Orville said. "When we focus only on our own thoughts, people around us may think we're being rude."

"Exactly," said Miss Eloise. "So when you're with a group of people, like in a class—"

"Or at a football game," Orville put in.

"Right. When you're in a group, you have to focus on what the other people are saying. Save your own thoughts for later, when you're alone."

Orville nodded. The One Who Is Innocent Until Proven Guilty would have to wait. "Miss Eloise?" he said. "Can we talk about how to figure out a motive?"

The teacher looked surprised. "A motive for what?"

"Just how to tell why someone does something," Orville explained. "I don't understand it."

"Hmm." Miss Eloise sank her two front teeth into her lower lip. She did this an average of six times per social skills class. "It's hard to understand what makes other people tick," she said. "In fact, that's hard for *everyone* to understand. So I think it may be a little too advanced for our class." She gave Orville an apologetic smile. "Maybe next year, okay?"

Orville counted five seconds. "Okay," he said.

Miss Eloise went back to the front of the room.

"Does anyone know what *faux pas* means?" she asked.

"It's French," said Drew Brody. She had one pigtail half unbraided. Drew braided and unbraided her hair ten times during every class. "It means 'false step.'"

Orville knew that Drew loved French as much as he loved planes. She would probably keep talking about French now for the rest of the class if Miss Eloise didn't stop her. "Thanks, Drew," Miss Eloise said quickly. "The term *is* French. But what it means these days is a social blunder."

Despite his best efforts, Orville felt his thoughts returning to The One Who Is Innocent Until Proven Guilty. He couldn't help it—social skills class was boring. Agatha always told him that social things were important, but they usually seemed pointless to him. He forced himself to concentrate on Miss Eloise. She had eighteen freckles on her left cheek. She was talking about social blunders.

"Who knows what to do after you burp?" she asked.

"Is burping a blunder?" asked Chris Pearson. "Why?"

"It's considered rude," Miss Eloise replied. She had twenty-one freckles on her right cheek. Burping was something that just happened sometimes. "Why is it rude?" Orville asked.

Miss Eloise smiled. "In some cultures, it's very polite to burp. In our culture, it's rude. This is one of those rules you'll just have to memorize."

Orville wrote it in his notebook: *Burping is a social blunder.* He had an entire list of social rules that didn't make sense—not even to Miss Eloise. But they were rules that he was expected to follow anyway. Sometimes Agatha added to his list.

"If you burp in front of someone else, you should apologize," Miss Eloise went on. "Finish your burp, and then say, 'Excuse me.'"

Orville wrote that all down. He didn't burp much, but he would try to remember.

"Another faux pas would be if you accidentally spill something," Miss Eloise said. "Like when you're at the dinner table and you spill some gravy when you're serving yourself. Or when you're at lunch in the cafeteria and you spill your drink."

"Why does that matter?" Drew asked. She was unbraiding her left braid.

"Sometimes it doesn't matter very much," Miss Eloise replied. "But if you spill something on another person, then it matters a lot."

"They yell," Orville said. Stu Frysley was always spilling things on people, and Agatha would always yell at him.

"They may, although that is also rude. So if you spill something on another person, you have to apologize," Miss Eloise said. "You say, 'I'm very sorry. It was an accident.'"

As Orville wrote that down, he remembered Samantha Boutry grabbing his arm in the mall. She had gotten ink on his sleeve. And she hadn't apologized. He raised his hand. "What if you didn't spill anything, but you rubbed something off onto someone?"

Miss Eloise bit her lip again. "You mean like mud or dirt?" she asked.

"Or ink," Orville said.

"Yes, that would follow the same rule," the teacher replied. "If you rub something onto another person, you have to apologize."

Orville wrote that down. Obviously Samantha Boutry needed some social skills classes too.

Chapter 9

"The scene of the crime," Agatha murmured, glancing around the burnt-out field house on Friday morning. She had asked Orville to meet her here before school. She'd tried to make it sound like they needed to do more investigating. But deep down, she knew it was because she was all out of ideas. Not to mention suspects.

Orville rode up on his bike and parked it carefully on the track that ran around the perimeter of the charred football field. He picked his way over the rubble of the field house until he got to Agatha. He looked her in the eyes. "Hi," he whispered.

"Hey. How was your skills class yesterday?" Agatha asked.

"Boring."

Agatha nodded. This was the conversation they had every Friday morning. Orville thought "social skills" equaled "pointless behavior." Agatha never told him this, but sometimes she thought he was right. It wouldn't kill people to care a little less about what everyone else thought of them, especially in middle school. At least John Q. wasn't as bad as Placid—*everyone* there seemed to be obsessed with their social standing.

"Samantha Boutry committed a faux pas," Orville added in a whisper.

Speaking of obsessed with status, Agatha thought wryly. Samantha was one of the worst offenders. "What did she do?" Agatha asked. "And when did you see her, anyway? She wasn't at your skills class."

Orville waited patiently for Agatha to stop talking. Then he held out his arm. The sleeve of his windbreaker had a big blotch on it. "She touched me at the mall when I went there and talked to Rachel Cruz," he whispered. "She kept holding on to my arm, and at one point, she smeared this ink on me."

Agatha leaned forward to take a better look. She couldn't get too close or Orville would freak out. But she didn't need a microscope to tell her what was on his jacket. The ink was a very distinctive purple color. "That's the shoplifter's special!" she cried.

"What?"

"That's what Uncle Irv calls it," Agatha explained. "It's from these big plastic clips that stores put on their merchandise. Then if someone steals the merchandise and tries to take the clip off, it explodes and spews ink all over the place."

Orville didn't say anything.

"You know, so whatever the person stole is ruined," Agatha added. "Because it's permanent ink. Uncle Irv keeps pestering Nana Wong to get some for the Trixie costumes at the store."

Orville still didn't say anything. "So, sorry, I guess your windbreaker is ruined," Agatha finished.

"I don't care," Orville whispered. "But Samantha was supposed to apologize for it, and she didn't."

"Wait a minute." Agatha had been so busy talking that she hadn't even realized the weirdest part of Orville's story. "If Samantha Boutry got ink on you, that means she must've had ink on herself."

"Yes," Orville agreed.

"But why would she have shoplifter ink on her? Unless . . ." Agatha's voice trailed off as she realized what had happened: Samantha had stolen something! She must've tried to take the tag off and gotten ink on herself. Then she'd grabbed Orville's arm and smeared it on him. "Did she really steal something?" she asked out loud.

"She was showing signs of paranoia," Orville whispered helpfully. "Looking over her shoulder a lot. According to the *Introduction to Psychology* textbook my mom gave me, that is a symptom of a paranoid mind."

"Or she was checking to make sure no one saw her talking to you," Agatha replied. "For Samantha, being seen with a John Q. kid would be worse than getting caught stealing." She turned to look at the blackened floorboards. "It's weird, though," she murmured.

"Samantha's obviously wealthy, like every other Placid kid. Why would she steal things?"

Orville kicked a charred piece of wood with his shoe. "What are we looking for?" he asked, still whispering.

Agatha realized that she was staring hard at the ground. She heaved a sigh and looked back up at her best friend. "I'm not really sure," she admitted. "But we're all out of suspects, so I figured maybe we could find some more evidence. This is where it all started, right? I was hoping we'd see something that we missed last time." Saying it out loud made her feel stupid. Why had she ever thought she and Orville would be able to solve this crime? They were just a couple of kids.

"I don't see anything new," Orville told her as he studied the remains of the room.

"I know," Agatha said. "Maybe we should just give up."

"What's going on here? Are you two lost?" a man's voice called out.

Agatha jumped in surprise. She hadn't heard anyone coming, but there was a man standing just outside the field house. "No, sorry," she said hastily. "We were just looking for . . . something."

The man stepped inside the charred building. He wore khakis and a faded sweater. His dark hair was shot through with gray. "You won't find much here, I'm afraid," he told Agatha. "It really is completely destroyed." He gazed around the field house as if he couldn't quite believe his eyes.

"Are you one of the teachers at Placid?" Agatha asked.

The man shook his head. "I'm the groundskeeper," he replied. "Well, I *was* the groundskeeper. There are no grounds to keep now."

Agatha gasped. "You mean because of the fire?"

He nodded sadly. "They'll reseed in the spring, but there's no point in keeping someone on the payroll when there's no work to be done. The reseeding will be done by a seed company, and they won't need a groundskeeper again until the end of the summer, when the grass has grown in."

"That's terrible. I can't believe you lost your job because of this," Agatha said. "How long had you been working here?"

"Oh, not long at all," he said. "I came in to pick up my pay." He held up an envelope. "This is my first—and last—check."

Agatha looked at Orville to see what he thought of this poor man's situation. But as usual, she couldn't read her friend's expression. Orville was just staring at the groundskeeper intently.

"I'm so sorry," she said again. Even though she knew that their prank hadn't started the fire, she couldn't help feeling responsible. "I'm sure you'll find another job soon."

"I doubt it," he replied. "I was out of work for a year before I got the job here. Who knows how long it will be this time?"

He didn't sound like he was complaining. He just sounded sad. Agatha thought about all the times her uncles and aunties had discussed the bad job market. She'd never really understood what they were talking about before.

"It's horrible," she said sincerely. "The fire ruined everything."

"That's true." The groundskeeper kicked at a pile of ashes with his toe. "I wanted to take one last look around. They're going to bulldoze what's left of this building next week."

Agatha felt hopelessness overtake her. Once the field house was gone, they would never find a new suspect. And she would never prove she and Orville were innocent.

"This place just shouldn't have gone up so fast," the groundskeeper said thoughtfully. "From what I hear, it practically exploded."

Agatha nodded. "We were there. It did explode."

"You have detached earlobes," Orville added in his normal voice.

Even Agatha was taken aback by that one. "Excuse me?" the groundskeeper said, his eyebrows raised.

"Detached earlobes," Orville repeated. "And a widow's peak. And your index finger is approximately three millimeters longer than the norm."

"Well, you're right about the ears and the widow's peak," the man said slowly. "But I'm afraid I never noticed my extra-long finger."

"Samantha Boutry shares all of those characteristics," Orville whispered to Agatha.

Now the groundskeeper chuckled. "That's probably because she's my daughter," he said. "Are you friends with Sam?"

"No," Orville said.

"We're just sort of, um, acquaintances," Agatha put in quickly. "She's older than us and she's so popular and everything."

"She always has been," Mr. Boutry said proudly.

Agatha liked Samantha's father. She didn't want to be rude to him. But if she had to stand here talking to him for one more second, her head might explode. There were too many amazing, mind-blowing thoughts running through it!

"We have to go now," she said. "Um, we're late for class."

"No, we aren't," Orville whispered.

"We will be," Agatha shot back, giving Mr. Boutry a big smile. "Good luck with your job hunt."

She bolted out of the ruined field house and jogged over to where she'd dropped her bike on the ground. Orville followed. "We have 38.7 minutes before school starts," he whispered. "The ride from John Q. to Placid has taken us an average of thirty-one minutes this week. It's only logical to assume that the ride in the opposite direction will take the same amount of time. So—"

"Orville, I know," Agatha interrupted. "I was lying to get away from Mr. Boutry."

"Oh," Orville whispered.

"Don't you get it?" Agatha cried happily. "*Samantha* set the fire!"

"Wait!" Orville said in his normal voice. "You told me I couldn't accuse her without evidence."

Agatha's mouth dropped open. What was he talking about? "I never said you couldn't accuse Samantha," she said. "Samantha was never even a suspect!"

"I know," Orville replied, back to whispering. "But I knew she set the fire."

Speechless. Agatha was speechless, even though Jack was nowhere in sight. Was it possible that Orville had known all along who their culprit was?

"Why didn't you tell me this sooner?" Agatha asked.

"You said we weren't allowed to accuse a suspect unless we had motive and evidence," Orville whispered. "I don't have either of those for Samantha."

"But . . ." She didn't know where to begin. Samantha had a *huge* motive, and Orville still didn't seem to get it. "Orville, we just discovered a motive for Samantha."

He was silent. Agatha knew that meant he had nothing to say.

"Listen," she said. "You know how Samantha is always making snotty comments about what people wear or what they look like? The way she made fun of Tina Gore for being from Bottomless Lake?"

Orville shrugged. He never noticed things like snotty comments because he didn't really know what it meant to be snotty.

Agatha started over. "Samantha wants to be popular. In fact, she *is* popular. But if the other kids at her school found out that her father was the groundskeeper, she wouldn't be popular anymore."

"Why not?" Orville whispered.

"Because . . .well, because being a groundskeeper is embarrassing to someone from Placid. It's almost as bad as being a janitor."

"What's bad about it?"

Agatha sighed. She wasn't even sure *she* knew—how was she supposed to explain it to Orville? "There's nothing really bad about it," she said. "Mr. Boutry was only trying to have a job so he could support his family. Being a groundskeeper or a janitor is a job."

"Like training pigs or running a souvenir store," Orville whispered.

"Right. But the kids who go to Placid are all pretty wealthy," Agatha said. "And it seems like they mostly care about things like who has money and who doesn't. At least, that's what Samantha cares about."

"So?"

"So parents in Placid probably all have high-paying jobs. And being the groundskeeper isn't a very high-paying job. If Samantha's friends found out that her dad was working here, they would use it as an excuse to make fun of her."

Orville blinked. He didn't answer.

"She was probably shoplifting things at the mall because her family doesn't have the kind of money they used to," Agatha said. "But Sam is afraid to let her friends know that money is tight, so she steals stuff and pretends she bought it."

"Why is that a motive to set a fire?" Orville whispered.

"If Samantha's friends saw her father mowing the grass on the football field, they would know he worked here. And they'd make fun of her and be mean to her. So she burned the field. No field, no groundskeeper, just like her dad said. She knew he'd get fired. And then nobody would find out that her family is broke."

Orville was silent for a while. Agatha was too. She figured that he would need some time to absorb all this. She could hardly believe it herself. Samantha had made her own father lose his job. That was really low.

"I don't get it," Orville whispered.

"I know," Agatha said. "It's despicable."

"No, I don't understand," Orville replied. "I think not understanding people's motives runs in my family."

Agatha thought about that. It seemed entirely possible, at least on his dad's side. "Well, never mind," she said. "You can take my word for it—Samantha has a big, big motive. And she had opportunity. She wasn't giving commentary during the halftime show. Chet was running the camera, but that doesn't mean Sam was with him."

"We still don't have any evidence," Orville pointed out in a whisper.

Agatha studied her best friend. The way he looked at people was so different from the way she did. She would never have known that the groundskeeper was Samantha's father, but Orville guessed it just by looking at him. And he'd known that Richie Cruz pulled the Sharks' halftime prank the same way. "You know, Orville," she said. "I bet we do have evidence. I bet it's right there in your brain."

"That seems highly unlikely," Orville replied.

"You said you've known all along that it was Samantha," Agatha said. "*How* did you know?"

Orville shifted his weight from one foot to the other—a sure sign that he was agitated. "I don't know," he whispered. "It was just obvious that she did it, but when you asked for a motive or evidence, I didn't have any."

"But you looked at her and you knew she was the perp, right?"

"Right."

"Okay, let's think about this logically," Agatha said. "You knew Richie pulled the Placid prank, and when I asked you about it, you were able to come up with all sorts of little details that led you to that conclusion."

Orville nodded.

"Okay, so we just need to figure out what little details you noticed about Samantha," Agatha decided.

"Like her father, she has a widow's peak and detached earlobes," Orville whispered. "Although in her case the earlobes are thicker. The widow's peak seemed more pronounced on Mr. Boutry. Samantha's hair falls forward, obscuring the peak, which may account for the variation in appearance. I would need to take precise measurements and adjust for the difference in diameter of her head versus her father's—"

"Stop!" Agatha cried. "Maybe we can narrow it down. When did you first know that she was the arsonist?"

"The day we talked to her in the TV station office," Orville whispered.

"Good. Tell me everything you noticed that day."

"Samantha drinks her water at an average of two sips per minute. Her eyelids are three shades darker than the skin on the rest of her face. I've allowed for the possibility of eye shadow, although the color was in the range of possible skin tones. She had a Band-Aid on the back of her hand. It was a small circular one with one edge peeling up. . . ."

Agatha listened carefully to the list of strange little things that Orville had noticed. She tried not to think about the kinds of weird stuff he must know about *her*. Instead she quickly ran each new detail through her mental perp checker to see if it could possibly be used as evidence against Samantha.

". . . the red socks matched the red sweater. Her left hand was in the pocket of her sweater ninety-two percent of the time we were in the room. When her hand was out, she tried to keep it behind her back. The sweater had six strands of Samantha's hair stuck to it—"

"Hold on a sec," Agatha said. "Did you say she was trying to hide her hand?"

"Her hand was rarely in sight," Orville replied.

"That's weird. Did you ever get a look at her hand?"

"Yes."

Of course he did, Agatha thought. *Orville obviously sees everything!* "What did you notice about it?" she asked aloud.

"I noticed that the disproportionate length of her index finger was the same on both hands. Her left hand had a paper cut on the thumb and the nail of her ring finger was jagged."

"That's it!" Agatha cried. She would've hugged Orville except it would freak him out. "You are a genius!"

Orville sighed. "I don't get it."

"Her nail was broken. That's practically a felony for a girl like Samantha. She has to have perfectly manicured nails at all times or else her friends will make fun of her."

"Maybe that's why she was so excited about buying the nail files and sticky nail things at the mall," Orville whispered.

"Huh?" Agatha asked. *I wonder how many times I say "Huh?" in a typical conversation with Orville?* she thought. She'd have to ask him that later.

"The night she got ink on me. She wanted to show me all her nail polish and manicure stuff. She said she had to have different color polish than everyone else."

"You didn't tell me that."

"I didn't care about it."

"So she bought a new nail file set because her nail was broken." Agatha dug around in her backpack until she found the Baggie with the turquoise plastic in it. "And the reason she needed a new nail file was that she lost her old one . . . in the field house!"

Orville peered at the piece of plastic. "That isn't a nail file."

"No, it's the handle of a nail file," Agatha said. "As soon as you mentioned nail files, I realized that. Cousin Eleanor has one just like it."

"Samantha's new nail file set did have plastic handles," Orville whispered. "They were pink and sparkly. And she told me that she needed a new set because she lost her old one. Plus the handle of her old nail file was blue in color. So was the handle of her hairbrush. I saw her give them to Chet at the snack shack. He put them in his pocket."

"See?" Agatha cried. "I knew you had the evidence in your amazing brain!" She pulled the other Baggie out of her backpack. "And this slit in the gardening supply bag? I thought it looked like someone had stabbed the bag with a spoon and dragged it along. But it wasn't a spoon. It was a nail file." She grinned at her best friend. "And that's how you knew she was our fire starter!"

"Samantha's nail was ragged because her nail file was destroyed in the fire?" Orville sounded like he were figuring this out as he spoke.

"Uh-huh. She probably tore her nail the next day at school and hadn't had time to replace the nail file yet. That's when we saw her and she was trying to hide her hand."

"Is that enough evidence?" Orville asked.

"I don't know," Agatha admitted. "Let's find out."

"We're going to be late," Orville whispered urgently as they biked back over to the front of Albert L. Placid Middle School. Students were hanging around outside and more school buses were pulling up the big circular driveway in front.

"This is worth being late for," Agatha told him. She dumped her bike near the bike rack and ran up the stone steps to the front door. Orville neatly chained his bike and followed her. From the top of the stairs, Agatha had a pretty good view of the kids pouring in. It seemed like most people were waiting outside as long as they possibly could. She couldn't blame them—the whole front lawn of the school was beautifully landscaped, with lots of little stone picnic tables and benches set up underneath the carefully pruned trees. John Q. didn't even have a front lawn. *If you go to school in a place like this, you start to think* everyone *has money*, Agatha thought. *Maybe Samantha is just trying to fit in.*

But that still wasn't an excuse for starting a fire, and Agatha knew it.

"What are we looking for?" Orville whispered.

"Samantha," she told him.

"She's approximately fifty feet away," he replied. "Under that palm tree."

Agatha peered at the place where Orville was pointing. Sure enough, there was Samantha with her snobby friends. As Agatha watched, they turned and began heading for the front door. So did a lot of the other people. "It must be almost time for the bell to ring," she said. "Just back me up."

Orville looked at her blankly.

Samantha's loud laugh cut through the noise of the crowd. She was on the steps, only ten feet away now. Agatha pushed her way through the other kids. "Sam!" she called. "Hey, Sam!"

Samantha looked right at her. Her eyes widened a tiny bit in recognition. Then she glanced away and kept on walking—right past Agatha and Orville. Agatha rolled her eyes. She'd expected Samantha to pull something like this. She would never acknowledge them in front of her Placid friends.

"We just met your dad," she called after Samantha.

Immediately Sam stopped walking.

"Come on, Orville," Agatha said. "Let's wait over here." She led the way to the side of the steps, out of the path of the kids trying to get into the building. She knew Samantha would come find them, and in less than a minute, she did.

"What do you want?" Samantha demanded. "Don't you have your own school?"

"Yes," Orville said. "And we're late."

Agatha pulled the Baggie with the turquoise plastic out of her backpack and handed it to Samantha. "We thought you might want this back," she said.

Samantha held the Baggie up between two perfectly manicured fingers. "What's this?" she asked. Agatha was sure Samantha's voice was twice as high as normal. Orville could probably tell her the exact percentage.

"It's what's left of your nail file," Agatha said triumphantly. "The one you used to slit open the gardening bags. You left it in the field house."

Samantha's face fell like a bad soufflé.

"And I'm guessing that if we went to your house, we'd find the rest of the manicure set—with handles made out of the exact same plastic."

Agatha drove the point home. Samantha was busted.

"Chemicals mixed with the chalk?" Orville asked.

Samantha nodded. She seemed smaller somehow. Just a regular girl.

Agatha frowned. She was supposed to be in charge of bringing down the perp. Now, suddenly, she had no idea what was going on. "Orville," she said. "What are you talking about?"

"I went into the field house the day before the game," Samantha said. "I just opened up all the bags that said Flammable on them and spilled the stuff out. And then I took one bag and dumped it into the barrel of chalk that they make the football yard lines with. The next morning, my dad put the chalk into the yard maker and spread the flammable stuff all over the field."

"That's why the fire was spreading in straight lines," Agatha realized.

"It was the only way I could be sure enough of the field would burn, not just the field house," Samantha said.

"You needed the field to be ruined or else your dad would still have his job," Agatha said.

"So what? It's good he got fired—now he can go get a normal job. He used to be the president of a bank. I want him to do that again." Sam glanced down at her feet. "He was humiliating me," she mumbled.

"I think you're the one who's humiliated him by turning into an arsonist," Agatha told her. "And you purposely set that fire at the time of our prank. You knew *we'd* get blamed."

Now Samantha looked angry. "No! I did it at halftime because I didn't want anyone to get hurt," she snapped. "The players wouldn't be on the field, and everyone in the stands would be watching. I knew lots of people would call the fire department the second they saw flames, and everyone would get away unharmed."

"Plus John Q. would get in trouble for it," Agatha said bitterly.

"Well, I couldn't let anyone find out that *I* did it," Samantha pointed out, using a bit of her I'm-a-Placid-princess attitude.

"How did you know about our prank?" Orville asked.

"I hung out with Stu Frysley," Samantha replied. "I saw him at Placid Pizza one day and he was bragging about being the prank secretary. So I just pretended to like him. Then, while he wasn't looking, I read about the prank in his notebook."

Orville turned to Agatha. "Does that mean Stu is a double agent?" he whispered.

"No, it just means he's an idiot," Agatha said.

Samantha sniffled. She had tears in her eyes. For one second, Agatha felt sorry for her. Agatha knew the allure of the silver bird of popularity. Samantha just wanted to hold on to her ticket. "Let's get this over with," she said. "Where's the principal's office at this place?"

"Why?" Samantha asked.

"Because you're going to go in there to tell your principal that you set that fire," Agatha said. "And we're going to watch."

Chapter 10

Orville's heart rate remained steady on the ride back to Bottomless Lake. This was surprising, given that they were half an hour late for school already. Usually in such a situation, his heart rate would climb at least half a percent. And that was in addition to the general increase that leaving Placid caused.

I must be relieved, he thought. Agatha certainly was. Now that Samantha had confessed to setting the fire, everything could go back to normal. Lissa would be reinstated as class president. Jack and Nathan would be back on the football team.

Orville didn't see why that mattered now that the season was canceled. But Agatha assured him that it was very important. Even more important than that, things wouldn't happen at school that made Agatha furious and humiliated and want to cry.

Yes, it would be nice to have things back to normal again. Normal would be more like living in Placid. If only he could talk to Agatha again instead of whispering or singing. But Ms. Winogrand said he wasn't allowed, and Orville knew he had to listen.

They chained their bikes to the overcrowded

bike racks and headed toward the John Q. doors.

"You know, we make a good team," Agatha told him. "You notice things and I interpret them. It's perfect."

Orville counted the seconds. She began speaking again after three. "But I still don't get why you were asking everyone those weird questions all week. I mean, you knew it was Samantha all along. So why the interrogations?"

"You told me I had to figure out a motive for Samantha, but I don't understand other people's motives. They never seem based on logic," he whispered

Agatha snorted. That usually meant she agreed with him.

"So I was using other people as test subjects. I thought if I could understand their motives for doing what *they* did, maybe I could figure out Samantha's motive for setting the fire as well."

"And how did that work for you?" Agatha asked, pushing open the only functioning side of the double door.

"It didn't work at all."

"There you two are!" Mr. Ben, the secretary, stood beaming down at them. "Principal Rothman wants to see you in his office right away!"

As they followed him down the hall, Orville leaned closer to Agatha. "We'll probably get more detention for being late."

She laughed. "Orville, we're not getting in trouble,"

she said. "Didn't you see how Mr. Ben was smiling?"

"Yes," Orville whispered. But he didn't see what Mr. Ben's face and their getting in trouble had to do with each other.

"Ms. Wong, Mr. Wright," Principal Rothman greeted them as they walked into his office. "You two are the heroes of the day. I just got off the phone with Principal Eiselin from Albert L. Placid Middle School. I hear you were already over there this morning."

"Yes. We're sorry we're late, but we wanted to make sure Samantha confessed to the proper authorities," Agatha said, standing a tiny bit straighter.

"That's a good reason for tardiness," Principal Rothman said. He straightened his tie, which had a giant Trixie on it. Trixie's nails were silver, which Orville knew was not the official Trixie nail color. According to the first account of a Trixie sighting, she was a reptilian monster with gray scales that looked purplish at night. She had double rows of teeth and sharp black claws. Black, not silver, and—

"Mr. Wright?"

Orville looked up. Agatha and the principal were both staring at him. Obviously he had been lost in his own thoughts again.

"You can go to class now," Principal Rothman said.

"Okay." Orville followed Agatha to the door. She turned back suddenly and Orville nearly walked into her—*again*. He would have to start keeping count of how many times she did that.

"Mr. Rothman?" she asked. "Can Orville have your permission to talk to me?"

"Excuse me?" The principal's eyebrows lifted.

"It was a detention rule, us not talking to each other, and Orville takes rules really seriously. But since detention is canceled now, obviously we can talk again. Orville will need to hear it from someone official," Agatha said without taking a breath.

"Oh." The principal's eyebrows were still lifted. "Okay. You can talk to each other."

"Thanks!" Agatha led the way out of the office and into the hall.

"Boy, I'm glad I can stop whispering," Orville said. "It hurt my throat."

As they walked to class, the PA system gave its usual shriek. "This is Principal Rothman," it said. "I'd like to tell you all that a Placid Middle School student took responsibility this morning for burning up our football field. We'd never have known of this crime without our own intrepid detectives, the team of Wright and Wong. Thanks to them, our football team will be playing on the field again by next season."

"Cool!" Agatha gave Orville a thumbs-up. "We're intrepid!"

He nodded. When they reached his classroom, he

turned to go in. Then he remembered. "Bye, Agatha," he called.

By lunchtime, school was an utterly different place. No one was shooting dirty looks or spitballs at Agatha. The notes in her locker were all congratulation notes. And Lissa had actually hugged her and said they should hang out.

Best of all, after her fourth-period class, Jack was waiting for her in the hall. "Hey!" he cried. "You did it!" He raised his hand for a high five.

Remember, as little talking as possible, she thought. She raised her hand and slapped his, a tingle shooting through her as their palms touched.

"I knew you guys could figure it out," he said. "You're both really smart."

Jack is complimenting me! Agatha thought. *Somebody pinch me, because I must be dreaming!*

"So listen, I wanted to talk to you," Jack said. He stepped closer and lowered his voice. Agatha thought her heart might actually explode.

"I talked to Coach Pettit," Jack went on.

He seemed to be waiting for her to say something. Agatha decided to follow Orville's example. "Okay," she said.

"It was just like you thought. Coach was really cool. He didn't care about me being color blind. He said he'd talk to the coach at the high school and they'd find a way to work around it."

"That's great, Jack," Agatha said. And she meant it. She'd inspired him! She'd gotten her crunch over a major life hurdle!

"Yeah. So anyway, thanks, Abigail." Jack turned and ambled off down the hallway, taking Agatha's happiness with him.

Abigail? After all they'd been through this past week, he still didn't know her name?

"Your eyebrows are pulling toward each other," Orville said as he came toward her. She turned to face her best friend. His face was blank, the way it always was when he was thinking. "That means you're . . . sad?"

"Yeah." Agatha began walking with Orville toward the cafeteria. "I am a little sad. Was that from your social skills class?"

Orville nodded. "After you pointed out Mr. Ben's smile, I decided to study my old notes about facial expressions and what they can tell me about people's emotions."

"Well, it's working," she said. "You figured *me* out."

"I want to understand how you're feeling all the time," Orville told her. "You can have half of my tuna-and-sea-monster-slime sandwich. That will cheer you up."

"Thanks, buddy" Agatha said. "But I'm not sure. . . ." Her voice trailed off as she stepped through the cafeteria door. The whole room fell silent as one face after the other turned in their direction. Pretty much every person in the room was staring right at Agatha and Orville. It was like the worst nightmare she could ever have.

And then . . . everyone in the cafeteria started clapping. All of them. Even *Stu!*

Agatha's mouth dropped open. She couldn't think of a single word to say, but that was fine, because everyone just kept cheering as Orville led the way to their usual table.

Agatha was grinning from ear to ear by the time they sat down. They were popular! *Outrageously*, stupendously, terrifically popular.

"You're smiling and seventy percent of your teeth are showing," Orville commented. "That means you're happy?"

Agatha smiled even wider at her best friend. "Couldn't be happier." She snagged a half of Orville's sandwich and held it aloft. "Here's to us, Wright and Wong, the coolest detectives in school!"